JESSICA BECK

CAST IRON COVER-UP

THE THIRD CAST IRON COOKING MYSTERY

Cast Iron Cover-Up
Copyright © 2015 by Jessica Beck All rights reserved.
First Edition: October 2015

No part of this book may be reproduced, scanned, or distributed in any printed or electronic form without permission. Please do not participate in or encourage piracy of copyrighted materials in violation of the author's rights. This is a work of fiction. Names, characters, places, and incidents either are the product of the author's imagination or are used fictitiously, and any resemblance to actual persons, living or dead, business establishments, events, or locales is entirely coincidental.

Recipes included in this book are to be recreated at the reader's own risk. The author is not responsible for any damage, medical or otherwise, created as a result of reproducing these recipes. It is the responsibility of the reader to ensure that none of the ingredients are detrimental to their health, and the author will not be held liable in any way for any problems that might arise from following the included recipes.

To P,
For always being there for me, and so very much more!

When a group of five college students visit the Cast Iron Store and Grill, Pat and Annie learn that they are in town searching for Jasper Blankenship's long-lost fortune. Instead of finding buried treasure, though, one member of the group is murdered at the dig site. Did one of the students kill their companion, or did someone from town find out what they were up to and decide to go for the gold themselves?

CHAPTER 1

FIVE PEOPLE CAME TO MAPLE Crest looking for buried treasure. What they found instead was murder.

CHAPTER 2: PAT

"Excuse me, sir. Do you have any picks?" a young man asked me as he approached the front counter of the Cast Iron Store and Grill—the Iron for short—the business I run with my twin sister, Annie. He looked to be in his early twenties and had broad shoulders and a mop of dark hair lightened by the sun.

"Toothpicks are beside the paper plates, guitar picks are by the kazoos, and our ice picks are in the hardware section."

"Sorry, I should have been a little more specific. I mean pickaxes," he said with a grin. "A toothpick or a guitar pick would be worthless for what we're doing, and an ice pick wouldn't be much better."

"Thanks for clarifying that," I said. "Come with me and I'll show you what we've got."

As I led him to the section in question, I noticed that the restaurant area of our store had a nice collection of customers at the moment, and Annie was busy feeding them all. Normally, I knew just about our entire clientele with the exception of a straggler every now and then or someone who lost their way from the Interstate, but most of this group was all new to me. Two girls and two boys were still eating, and they all looked to be in their late teens and early twenties. Two of them had well-worn backpacks, and from a bit of the conversations I'd overheard earlier, they were all more educated than most of the kids who usually hung around the Cast Iron. "Are you guys on some kind of field trip from college or something?" I asked him.

"I guess you could say that," he replied, offering me a hand stained with red clay, some still stuck under his ragged fingernails. He might be a student, but it was clear that he wasn't afraid to get his hands dirty. "I'm Henry, by the way. I suppose the best way to put it is that we're here performing a little practical application of our classwork."

"Nice to meet you, Henry. I'm Patrick Marsh, but everybody calls me Pat. Are you all geologists, then?"

"You'd think so, wouldn't you?" he asked with a grin. "But that's just about the only field we don't have with us. I'm the historian of the group, Marty is our cartographer, Gretchen is a mining engineer, Peggy is an archeology major, and Bones is pre-med, at least this semester. He has a habit of changing majors every semester or two, which might explain why he's a twenty-five-year-old sophomore."

"Is he along to patch you up if you get into trouble?" I asked. Henry was easy to talk to, and I found his openness refreshing.

"No, Bones is financing this expedition, or at least his father is. Bones has more money than he knows what to do with, and just between us, I think his pop is just happy that he's interested in doing something besides sliding through life."

"I've had friends like that myself," I said. We were at the tool section, and I showed him the pick I kept in stock.

Henry hefted it in his hands, and then he studied the wood grain of the handle and the markings on the metal section of the pick. "This looks like it's pretty well made," Henry said, clearly surprised to find it in my store.

"We believe in offering the best quality normal folks can afford," I said. "I know you can buy better tools, but not nearby, and at nowhere near what we charge for them."

"I believe it. Do you have any more of these in stock?"

I rarely sold more than a pickaxe a season, so his question surprised me. "I believe I might have one or two more in back."

"We'll take them, and these, too." Henry said as he added two top-of-the-line shovels as well.

On a hunch, I grabbed a sluicing pan I kept on hand for tourists and asked, "How about one of these?" After all, his purchases weren't exactly the norm for visiting college students, and besides, what else would his group need shovels and pickaxes for?

"Is that for gold panning?" he asked. "I've read about them, but I've never actually seen one." He twirled it in his hands. "It's just plastic, isn't it?"

"True, but that doesn't mean that it won't do the job."

"Is there really native raw gold around here?" It was pretty clear that Henry didn't know, which dampened my original theory that they were in town prospecting. A small amount of gold had been found in our area not long after a real mother lode was discovered on the Reed Farm near Charlotte in 1799, but it had never been enough for even the slightest rush to Maple Crest.

"I guess you're not looking for gold then, are you?" I asked him with a grin as I put the pan back on the pile of others.

"Not exactly," he said with an odd smile.

"Emeralds?" I asked. Our part of North Carolina had produced some nice gemstones in the past, but to my knowledge, none of them had ever surfaced around Maple Crest.

"No."

Henry had grown surprisingly reticent all of a sudden, and I wondered if I'd pushed him too far with my questions. "Sorry, I didn't mean to pry."

"You didn't," Henry answered. "I'm just not supposed to talk about it," he added as the young man he'd identified as Bones approached us.

"What are you up to now, Henry?" the short and dark-haired young man of the group asked.

"Just picking out some new equipment, Bones," Henry said, deferring to the financial backer of the trip.

Bones frowned for a moment before he spoke again. "I thought we agreed we were going to just get food and fuel in Maple Crest."

"I know, but this is quality stuff," Henry protested. "Take a look at it."

"I'm sure it is," Bones said, and then he replaced everything Henry had pulled off the rack, out of order. "We're set, though."

"Bones, I get that your dad is backing us, but we could really use these."

"You know, if you aren't happy with the arrangements, you can always head back to school early, Henry. No one will hold it against you," Bones said. He spoke in a friendly manner, but there was no warmth in his voice or his words.

"No, thanks. I'm staying," Henry said, casting his gaze down. "Sorry for the trouble, Pat."

"It's no trouble at all," I said, trying to resist the urge to immediately put everything back into its proper place. "We're here if you need us."

"Thanks," Henry said.

"Yes, thank you," Bones added before turning back to his associate. I called him that because it was pretty clear that the two young men weren't friends. "Henry, why don't you go rejoin the group?"

The historian nodded, and I expected Bones to go as well, but he stayed right beside me. "I trust you'll keep this to yourself, Pat."

"What, the fact that you and your group aren't here looking for gold, but that you're obviously digging for something of value?" I asked with a grin. I hadn't been able to help myself. This guy was using his father's money like a club, and I didn't like it, not one little bit.

"Henry told you that?" Bones asked, glancing back long enough to give the young man an icy stare before he looked back at me.

It was time to backpedal a little. "No, of course not. He was looking at picks and shovels, though, and he wouldn't be the first customer we ever had around here interested in buried treasure of one sort or another. I doubt you'll find any, but I still wish you all the best of luck. From what I've heard, just below the waterfall at Emerson's Creek is the best place for sluicing if you change your mind and decide to go after gold after all."

"Thank you for the tip," Bones said.

He turned to go, and I felt bad about putting Henry in a precarious position. I'd only spoken with him a few minutes, but I'd liked his easygoing attitude from the start. "Henry didn't breathe a word to me about what you were up to."

"Apparently he didn't have to," Bones said.

One of the girls in the group, a tall, lithe redhead, handed something to Bones. "Here's the bill for the food. The woman working at the lunch counter said that you should pay up front."

"Thanks, Peg. Tell Marty and Gretchen that I'd like to get started soon," Bones said as he watched the last two members of their party finishing their meals. Marty was heavyset, while Gretchen looked more like a hummingbird, small and petite, but very serious.

"I don't know where Gretchen puts it," Peggy answered with a grin.

"At least there's no question where Marty does," Bones said a little meanly.

"Bones, be nice," Peggy said, trying to force a smile.

"Sorry," Bones said, but there wasn't much energy in it. He turned back to me. "Where do I pay this bill?"

"I can check you out up front," I said.

The bill came to twenty-eight dollars and seven cents, and Bones handed me a hundred-dollar bill.

I got his change together and tried to hand it to him, but he grinned at me and said, "You can keep it."

"That's way too much for a tip," I protested as I tried to give him the money again.

"It's not just for the food. I'd be most appreciative if you didn't share what you learned with anyone else."

"I'm not exactly sure that I learned a blessed thing about what you're doing in town, but even if I did, I don't make it a habit of gossiping about my customers," I said as I finally managed to force the money into his hands.

Bones shrugged, and then he jammed it all into the tip jar. "Much obliged."

I wasn't going to be stupid about it. If he wanted to leave us a massive tip, I was sure the Humane Society would appreciate it. That was where all of our tips went at the moment, into a direct donation to one of the causes my sister and I cared about. Bones hadn't bought my silence, though. As soon as the first opportunity arose, I was going to tell Annie exactly what I'd seen and heard so I could see what she thought of it. I was curious to get my sister's take on the situation, but it wasn't until four hours later that I got the chance, when we were finally closing the Iron for the day.

CHAPTER 3: ANNIE

"Wow, I must have really impressed somebody with my culinary skills today," I said as I counted out the money in the tip jar at the end of our workday. "Pat, what's going on? I'm well aware of how good I am at running the grill, but even *I* don't think I merit this much."

My twin brother frowned as he looked at me. "Annie, if you don't mind, I'll wait and tell you all about it after Skip leaves for the day."

Skip Lawson was our only other full-time employee, a young man who considered himself the next big entrepreneur. If asked, he'd tell anyone about his grand scheme, even as he restocked the dog food we sold in Pat's section, an area that was part hardware and part grocery store. Edith Bost ran the post office and worked hours all her own, so she'd left for the day quite a bit earlier. As for me, I operated the grill in back, using cast iron whenever I could, doing my best to satisfy the appetites of folks in four counties with my offerings.

Skip must have heard his name mentioned. "What about me? Am I getting a raise, or are you firing me?" he asked with a grin. "Either way, I'm good."

"Pat was just about to tell you that you could take off early for the day," I told him with a grin.

"Seriously?" Skip asked as he looked expectantly at my twin brother.

"Sure. Why not?" Pat asked him, ever being the good sport. I couldn't imagine a better brother, and I'd gotten pretty lucky in the big sister department, too. Kathleen was our local sheriff, and though she still tried to mother us both on occasion, normally she was a pretty neat lady to be around.

After Skip was gone for the day, I asked Pat, "*Now* will you explain why you're being so cryptic?"

"Only if you help me restock the canned goods," Pat replied. "I was going to have Skip do it, but he seems to have been relieved of his duties."

"I'll make you a deal. I'll work if you talk," I told him. I helped Pat out occasionally up front, but mostly that part of the Iron was my brother's domain. He could cook, at least a little, but he mostly left the grill to me. It was a perfect arrangement, and neither one of us had any desire to change a system that worked just fine the way it was.

"Sold," he said. The boxes were already open, so it was simple to match the product with the label as I shelved green beans, peas, corn, and a variety of other canned goodies we carried.

"Pat, it feels as though I'm working, but you're not talking," I said.

"What were we discussing again?" he asked me, grinning.

"You're not getting senile on me, are you?"

"How can I be, when you're clearly so much older than I am?" Pat asked, still smiling.

I was in fact seven minutes older than my brother, enough to make our births occur in the a.m. and p.m. Our father had thought it would be cute to give us those initials, so I'm Annie while he's Pat. Mom had indulged him whenever she could, and their relationship had been a strong one right up to the minute they'd both been killed by a drunk driver, dying side by side and, according to the police, almost simultaneously. I knew that neither one of them had been in any hurry to die, but if they could have picked their personal departure dates, I was certain that they would have chosen to go together. Seeing parents so much in love had made it hard for me and my siblings to find anything close to that ourselves, but there was hope at the moment, at least for Pat and me. But that was another story altogether, and I needed information at the moment. "Just tell me what's going on, Pat."

"The tip was not so much for your excellent food as it was to ensure my silence," Pat said.

"That answer generates more questions than answers," I said.

I'd momentarily stopped working, something that hadn't escaped my brother's attention. "Don't stop now. Keep it up, Annie, and you'll be finished in no time."

"So will you if you don't make this story dance."

Pat could tell that he'd pushed me just about as far as he dared, something that had taken me years to teach him. "I'm not supposed to say anything, but that group of college kids you served lunch to earlier is here on a treasure hunt."

"You're joking, right?"

"No, Bones was pretty serious about it. The brat even tried to bribe me with his change from a hundred. Can you believe that?"

"I'm not a bit surprised. The entire time he and his group were eating, he must have reminded them all half a dozen times that without his backing, none of them would be there."

"Not a particularly nice kid, is he?"

"I'm not a fan," I admitted. "Do they think they're going to find a new vein of gold around here? Better folks than them have tried and failed."

"I thought so at first, but now I'm not so sure," Pat admitted.

"Why is that?" I asked, discarding one box and picking up another. I felt as though I was painting Tom Sawyer's fence, but I really did want to know what that group was up to.

"Henry told me everyone's specialty. Among them, they have a historian, a cartographer, an archeologist, a mining engineer, and a pre-med student."

"They could still be looking for gold as a hobby," I said.

"I forgot to mention something. Henry implied that they were each chosen to use the skills they'd been learning in school. So tell me this. Why would they need a cartographer? Everyone knows exactly where our only gold strike was. Shoot, I even told them again myself. So why bring a historian, not to mention an archeologist? This is no simple hobby. Something's going on, but I haven't a clue what it might be about."

"I don't either, but I'd love to find out," I said.

"How do you propose we do that?" Pat asked me.

"Leave it to me, dear brother," I said. "I have my methods."

"I just bet you do," he said as he grabbed the last box. "Thanks for lending a hand."

"It might not have been the least I could do, but it was pretty darn close," I said with a smile. "Do you have any plans after work?"

"Like what, mowing the lawn?" he asked me.

"You live upstairs. You don't have a lawn," I reminded him.

"Then I probably won't have to do that, will I?"

"Are you seeing Jenna tonight?" Jenna Lance was the town vet and, as of just recently, my brother's new girlfriend.

"She's out of town at a conference for the next four days," Pat said. "How about you? Are you going out with Timothy?" I'd been dating the accountant and outdoorsman since the same time Pat had first gone out with Jenny, the timing purely a coincidence. Timothy had bought a large tract of land that abutted mine, so technically we were neighbors, though we were still separated by a great deal of dense woods. I had eighty-two acres myself, while he was the new and proud owner of fifty-seven.

"He's been taking a class in Franklin in timber-framing all week, but he's coming home tomorrow," I said. "He wants to use the joinery techniques in the cabin he's going to build."

"That sounds like it could be really cool," Pat said.

"I know. So, we both go years without having significant others in our lives, and now that we do, they both bail on us. Is it us, do you think?"

My brother grinned at me. "Well, not me, at any rate."

I threw an empty box at him, which he easily ducked. "You're going to have to aim better than that," Pat added.

"Who said I was trying to hit you? That was just a warning shot."

He laughed. "Got it. Would you like to grab something to eat with me? I know we spend all day together, but we really don't get much chance to talk, do we?"

"If you're not sick of my face by now, then I guess I could stand seeing yours a bit more, too," I answered. It was the closest thing to a compliment he was going to get out of me, and he knew it.

"Sounds like a plan. Where should we go?"

I was about to answer when someone was suddenly banging on our front door. I'd seen Pat lock it earlier, so I knew that as far as he was concerned, we were closed for the day, barring some kind of major emergency.

I was about to tell the young woman exactly that when I saw the blood on her hand that she'd been using a second before to beat on our front door.

CHAPTER 4: PAT

"Call Kathleen," I told Annie as I raced to the door. Peggy, the archeologist from earlier, was standing outside, and she was a total mess. She'd clearly been sobbing, judging from the trails of tears still streaming down her face, and there were smudges of blood on her shirt and cheeks as well as her hands.

"What is it?" I asked as I unlocked the door and opened it. "What happened?"

"It's Bones. I think he's dead," she said, sobbing again as she collapsed into my arms.

"Calm down and tell us what happened," I told her as Annie dialed our sister's number. "Take a deep breath, Peggy. You can do it."

"Okay," she said, doing her best to stifle her tears. "We were at the dig site, and I had to take my car and come into town for dinner supplies. It's my turn to cook something on the camp stove tonight, and Bones was mad at me for forgetting to buy groceries when we were in earlier. Anyway, I wasn't away for more than thirty minutes, but when I got back to the site, everyone was gone, even the tents and the van the others came in. At least that's how it looked at first. Then I saw Bones, lying face down in the newest hole we'd been working on."

"Where exactly is this dig site?"

Peggy frowned at my sister. "I'm sorry, but I can't tell you that."

"Why not?" Annie asked, clearly getting frustrated with the college student. "How are we supposed to help Bones if we don't know where he is?"

"We didn't ask the owner permission to dig there," Peggy said. "I told Bones we had to do it, but he wouldn't let me. I'm so sorry."

"Why are you apologizing to me?" Annie asked. And then, after barely a moment's thought, she asked, "It's on my land, isn't it?"

"Part of it might be," Peggy acknowledged. "Most of the land we're digging on belongs to some guy named Roberts, but you might own a little of it, too. There's no building of any kind on his land, so we thought it would be okay."

"You thought wrong," Annie said as she started for the front door.

"Where are you going?" I asked her, as if I even needed to.

"I'm going to see what's going on. You can stay here if you'd like and wait for Kathleen, but I'm going to go find out what happened on my land."

"I want to go back with you, too," Peggy said, pleading. "I shouldn't have taken off like that. I panicked! But if we go back, if it's not too late, I might be able to do something to help him."

"Call Kathleen and tell her where we're headed," Annie told me.

There was no need to, though.

Our big sister, who also happened to be the sheriff, was driving up as we all walked out onto the Iron's front porch.

"Is that blood?" Kathleen asked the moment she spotted Peggy. "It's not yours, is it?"

"It belongs to my friend, Bones," she said. "Please. You've got to help him."

"Where is he, in your car?" Kathleen asked as she started toward the vehicle in question.

"No, he's either on my land or Timothy's," Annie said. She'd made it a point of pride paying the two of us for our share of the land, even if it had put her in a financial bind to do it. Kathleen and I had wanted to gift the property to her outright, but Annie wouldn't hear of it, so we'd set up a payment plan, and every month, part of my twin sister's share of the business went to Kathleen and me. I hadn't spent a dime of the money she'd been paying me, but I couldn't speak for Kathleen.

"What are you talking about? What exactly is going on here?"

"That's what we need to find out," I said. "Peggy, I know you're in town digging around looking for something. If it's not gold or emeralds, then what is it?"

"Can we talk as we drive? Please?" she begged me.

I looked at Kathleen, who nodded. "We'll all go in my squad car. Annie, you can sit up front with me. Pat, why don't you ride in back with her?"

I agreed.

Once we were on our way, Kathleen asked, "Now tell me the truth. What exactly are you looking for?"

"Buried treasure," Peggy said.

"Maybe you'd better go back and start from the beginning," I suggested.

"Three months ago, Henry found some documents buried in a stack of old papers in an unrelated archive, and there was a map there, as well. It was written in some kind of code, but we believe there's a great deal of money buried around here that nobody knows about." Peggy interrupted herself by saying, "Hey, you missed the turn."

"She's going in the right direction. My place is up ahead," Annie said.

"Maybe so, but we've been coming in and out on that road." When Kathleen turned around and backtracked a thousand feet, I saw fresh ruts in the service road that accessed Timothy's land.

"Those tracks look new," I said to Annie. "Did you notice them before?"

"I just assumed Timothy made them," she said. "I can't believe five people were digging on our land and I missed it."

"Eighty-two acres is a lot of ground to cover, especially when you spend so much time at the Iron," I said.

"I didn't even smell a campfire," Annie protested.

"That's because we never had an open fire since we got here. We've been cooking on one of those little propane stoves from the start," Peggy said. "We were all so happy to get decent food at your place this afternoon, I felt really bad about not telling you what we were doing."

"If that's supposed to make me feel better, you're going to need to try a little harder than that," Annie said.

Kathleen raised an eyebrow toward our sister as we jounced along the bouncy path. It certainly couldn't be called a road. Compared to this, Annie's driveway was an interstate. We came to a bit of a clearing, and Annie said from the back, "This is where the old Blankenship homestead used to be."

"It's pretty amazing, isn't it?" Peggy said. "I haven't been able to afford to go on any digs of my own yet, but what we've found here so far is really cool."

"Why don't we save the dig report until after we see to your friend?" Kathleen had called the ambulance driver and told her where we were headed, and I could hear the siren behind us in the distance. As we got out, my older sister asked, "Now where exactly is this body?"

Peggy led us to an area where the old homestead had once stood. I'd seen it six months before on a hike with Annie, but now it looked as though an oversized gopher had moved in, with holes randomly dug all over the place. I glanced at the hand-laid stone foundation, which was now all that was left of what once must have been a pretty nice home, according to local folklore. Jasper Blankenship had been a wealthy man, or so everyone had assumed until he'd died and left his widow nearly penniless. She'd been forced to sell off most of the land her husband had acquired, and my family had bought a nice-sized chunk of it, where my sister was now living. As I looked around, I saw an old well and what had to be a family cemetery nearby, too.

Peggy walked over to a freshly dug hole, and I noticed that they'd cut the barbed wire that separated Timothy's land from Annie's. This excavation seemed to straddle the property line, and as we all leaned forward, I took a deep breath before I looked at the body.

There was just one problem, though.

Bones was gone.

CHAPTER 5: ANNIE

"I DON'T UNDERSTAND," PEGGY SAID AS she stared down into the shallow hole, and I saw Pat touch her shoulder gently to comfort her. My twin brother had a way of soothing people that I couldn't master, no matter how hard I'd tried in the past. Okay, if I was being honest with myself, I never really tried all that hard in the first place. Why should we both have to be so compassionate? One of us had to be a cold-hearted pragmatist, so why not me?

"Are you sure he was in *this* hole?" I asked her. "Maybe it was somewhere else."

"I'm telling you, he was right there," Peggy said, her voice edging into hysteria.

Kathleen stepped down into the shallow hole, which was no more than two feet deep. It was six feet by six feet wide, and there was no way that a body could be hiding anywhere in it.

"This has been freshly dug," our older sister said as she got close to the dirt, pinched some between her finger and thumb, and then rubbed it away.

"Of course it was," Peggy replied. "We just finished it this afternoon."

"I don't see any blood anywhere," Kathleen answered calmly as she studied the disturbed soil carefully.

"Not to mention a body," I added.

That earned me a reproving look from both of my siblings, but Peggy didn't even seem to realize that I'd said anything.

"This just doesn't make any sense," Peggy said as she looked around. "Where is everybody?"

"Are you sure they were here earlier?" Kathleen asked her, as though the college girl had completely lost her mind.

"I can vouch for that part, at least. Five of them came into the grill for lunch this afternoon," I said, "and Pat met them, too. They were real enough then."

"Tell me about your companions," Kathleen said.

The ambulance finally made it to us just as my sister spoke. "Hold that thought, and wait right here. All of you," she added, looking at me and Pat in turn.

"Where would we go?" I asked my brother after our older sister walked over to confer with the ambulance driver.

"Oh, I don't know, how about off looking for Bones's body in the woods?"

"I told you before, he was right here," Peggy said, suddenly snapping back to us. "I don't know what's happening." After pausing for a moment, she began yelling each of her friends' names in turn. "Henry! Marty! Gretchen! Where are you?"

"Why didn't you call out for Bones?" I asked her softly.

"You didn't see him," she said as she shuddered a little. "Even if he were still alive by some miracle, there's no way he'd be in any shape to call out to me."

"Where were you all staying?" I asked as I looked around. "There aren't any tents here, so I'm assuming that you had a place in town."

"No, Bones thought that might be too suspicious, so we all camped here. Some of us stayed in tents, but they're gone now. We had the camper van, too," she said. "It's obviously not here, either. They must have all just packed up and left."

"Taking the body with them?" I asked her.

"Maybe we should wait for Kathleen to come back before we question her any more," Pat said to me.

"I'm not sure we have that much time to waste," I said, and then I turned back to Peggy. "Do you happen to know the plate number of the missing van?"

"No, of course not. I drove my car down here with Henry, and the rest of them came with Bones. I don't even know what state it's registered in. There are cars from all over at school."

"At least we know who the van belongs to," Pat said.

"Sorry, but we don't know that, either. Bones borrowed it from a friend at school," Peggy said as she shook her head.

"Is there any chance you know the student's name he borrowed it from?" I asked her.

"Sort of, but it's not going to do you any good," she said.

"Why not?"

"We all call him Sniffles at school, because of his allergies," she said. "I don't know if I've ever even heard his real name."

"What are you three talking about?" Kathleen asked us sharply as she returned.

"The van some of them came in is gone, and so are their camping equipment and tools," I said. "We can't get a plate number, or even the owner's name, for that matter. Maybe they took the body with them when they left."

"They wouldn't do that!" Peggy protested.

"Not even to rush him to the hospital?" Pat asked her gently.

"Okay, maybe they'd do that," she allowed. "But where were they when I found Bones before?"

"Don't worry. We'll ask them that when we find them," Kathleen said before turning to the ambulance driver. "Sorry for the wild goose chase."

"No worries, Sheriff. We're on the clock either way."

"Do me a favor and check with the hospital when you get there," Kathleen requested.

"What exactly are we looking for?" the attendant asked.

"Could you describe him for us, please?" Kathleen asked Peggy.

"He's in his mid-twenties, he's short, and he has dark hair," she said.

"And he answers to Bones, if he's in any shape to answer to anything," I said.

Pat gave me one of his critical looks, but I just shrugged. Was anything I'd just said a lie?

"Peggy, do you happen to know his real name?" Kathleen asked her.

"I'm sorry, but I don't."

"Wonderful. We have a missing student, four of them, actually, and one of them is injured, if not deceased. The problem? We don't have anything to go on."

"Do you need us for anything else, Sheriff? If not, we'll keep you in the loop if we hear anything," the driver said.

Kathleen looked at the young woman for a moment, and then she said, "Why don't you take her with you, okay?"

"What? Why? I'm not hurt," Peggy protested.

"We need to get you checked out and cleaned up," Kathleen said reasonably. "You're not going to be able to help Bones until we take care of you. Besides, I need to know more about these friends of yours."

"You could hardly call them friends. Henry's the only one I even knew before this weekend," she said.

"Then we'll start with him," Kathleen said.

"What about us?" I asked our older sister. "What would you like Pat and me to do in the meantime?"

"You could always ride back to town with me," Kathleen suggested.

"Or we could look around a little since we're here," I said. "My place is just through those woods. We can head there when we're through. It might be worth a shot if we hang around and looked for clues."

"Don't worry about that. I'll have some of my people do that," Kathleen said.

"Sis," I said in a soft voice, "if he's out there somewhere, he could be in serious trouble. How about if we promise not to touch anything, and if we do find something of interest at all, including Bones, we'll let you know ASAP?"

"Pat, do you agree to that?" she asked our brother.

"Of course. We won't disturb the crime scene, if that's your concern."

"If it even is one," Kathleen said softly as the attendants gently led Peggy away to the ambulance.

"Are you saying that you don't believe her?" I asked our older sister.

"Think about it. All we have is this girl's word that something happened out here today. She needs to get a thorough examination before I take her back to my office."

"Do you think she's hurt?" I asked, thinking about the blood we'd found on her.

"Honestly, I think there's a chance that she's high," Kathleen admitted. "I've seen it before. If she's on drugs, they may be doing something to her mind."

"I don't know. She seemed awfully lucid to me," Pat said.

"Plus, if it's all in her mind, where did the blood come from?" I asked.

"That's a very good question," Kathleen replied. "If you find *anything*, particularly a blood trail, call me. Do you understand?"

"We do," Pat and I answered in unison.

"I just wish I could believe either one of you," Kathleen said as she shook her head slightly.

After Kathleen and the ambulance were gone, Pat and I started our search.

We had to be quick, since Kathleen's people were probably on their way, so every second had to count.

A part of me dreaded the idea of stumbling across a body, but it was something that we had to do on the slight chance that Bones was out there alone and in need of some immediate medical attention.

CHAPTER 6: PAT

"Why exactly were they digging all of these random holes?" Annie asked me as she peered down into yet another shallow depression.

"Peggy already told us that. They were looking for buried treasure," I reminded her.

"I know that, but what specifically?"

"Beats me," I asked as I looked around the open area of what had once been the main house's front yard. Annie and I had already scanned the surrounding woods, and neither one of us had found a single thread of evidence that Bones had ever been farther than the clearing we were now standing in. There were no holes in this particular part of the clearing, but I could see where the weeds and grass had been matted down in three large rectangles. "At least she wasn't lying about the tents," I said, spotting a few places where pegs had been driven into the earth and hastily pulled out. "The question is why did they take off so suddenly?"

"Having a dead body to deal with might be a pretty good reason," Annie said.

"Sure, but why take it with them?"

"Pat, they might not have realized that Peggy came back to the site. If they left Bones's body to do something else, she could have showed up when they were gone."

"What do you think could possibly be more pressing business than dealing with a dead body?" I asked her.

"Finding a place to hide it," Annie answered grimly.

"We don't even know if Bones is really dead or not," I reminded her.

"Maybe not, but it doesn't do us any good assuming that he's in the hospital, does it? The only way we're going to be productive here is to work off the premise that someone killed him."

"Okay. Let's say for a moment that's true. It sounds as though it was clearly a homicide, and I doubt they all did it together. So why did the others leave?"

"Maybe they don't know who the real killer is themselves," Annie suggested.

"I would think that would be even more reason to call the police instead of packing everything up and getting out of here. If we hadn't seen evidence to the contrary ourselves, and if the group hadn't been at the Iron earlier today, there's a good chance that no one would believe Peggy now. We met the others, at least some of them, so we know that she wasn't alone, but if Peggy hadn't shown up and led us here, would we have had any reason to believe that what we're seeing is anything but what it looks like?"

"What exactly does it look like?" my twin sister asked me.

"Like someone went a little crazy with a shovel. There are what, seven holes dug around the perimeter here? I thought they had some kind of map. Do these holes look a little too random to you, too?"

"Maybe the directions weren't as clear as Peggy made them sound. If there was room for interpretation, it could easily lead to something like this."

"I don't know. It looks like a lot of trouble to me," I said.

"Pat, if Blankenship buried his money somewhere on the property and they managed to unearth it, it could be worth a fortune. I can't imagine how much his gold and silver would be worth on today's market."

"Then again, it could all just be one big lie," I told her. "Let's assume that it's true, though. There's no reason to believe that it hasn't already been found, even if it was ever buried somewhere around here in the first place."

"I'm guessing they at least found something," Annie said.

"Why do you say that?"

"If Bones is indeed dead, then someone must have killed him for a reason," she answered.

"That's a good point. Okay, let's assume that everything Peggy told us was the unvarnished truth. I know Kathleen thinks the girl is high on something, but she didn't seem that way to me. What did you think?"

"That she'd seen something traumatic," Annie said. "Was she under the influence of anything but shock? I don't think so."

"So, we're agreed on that much, at least. Let's play out the scenario the way she's presented it. Peggy leaves to get food, and someone, unknown to the others or not, kills Bones for whatever reason. Maybe he found something of value, or perhaps he pushed one of the other kids a little too far. Either way, he's in the excavation, either dying or already dead. It's not unreasonable to believe that no one saw the murder take place. One swing of a pickaxe or a shovel, and Bones falls down into the hole. While it's not deep enough to bury him, his body could still be obscured from everyone else's line of sight if they weren't nearby when it happened."

"Then how did the killer get the others to abandon the site?" Annie asked me.

"I'm not sure. He, or she for that matter, could have told them someone was onto what they were doing out here, so they had to scram, and fast."

"How would the killer explain Bones's absence?"

"Maybe they claimed he wandered off, and they'd come back for him later. The point is that they got the others to leave, and in a hurry. Once most of the signs of their presence were gone, the murderer must have worried about something he'd left behind that might incriminate him."

"Or her," Annie reminded me.

"I can't keep saying 'him or her,' and 'they' sounds a little clunky. Let's just agree to call the killer a generic 'he' and leave it at that, unless you prefer the female pronoun."

"No, 'he' is fine with me," Annie said.

"I'm glad we at least got that settled," I answered. "So, the killer evacuates everyone else, but he leaves the body behind. Peggy shows up, finds Bones, and then understandably flees. As soon as she's gone, the killer comes back and retrieves Bones's body. It shouldn't be too tough getting it in the back of a van. Only what does he do with it then? He can't just chauffer it around town until he comes up with a convenient place to unload it."

"And the other three don't even realize what has happened. Are they in danger as well?" Annie asked me.

"Not if they don't find the body before the killer gets rid of it. If they do, then they become liabilities, and there will be a higher body count than we've got now."

"This open space alone will take forever to search," Annie said. "We can't just comb through the grass and weeds on our hands and knees. What we could use is a metal detector."

"If we find these kids, I've got a hunch they already have one," I said. "Why else would they dig in what looks to be a random pattern? The map must have brought them here, but I have a feeling that they weren't able to solve the cryptography completely. They should have brought a math major with them if they couldn't find someone good with puzzles."

"Why do you think they used a detector, Pat?"

"Look at the holes. They don't follow any kind of search grid I've ever heard of. Other than picking a spot and hoping to get lucky, I have a hunch that they used the detector and tried to find the buried money that way."

"Why two feet deep, though?" she asked me.

"Maybe that's as far as the treasure was buried, according to the documents Henry found. Who knows? It could simply mean that's as deep as their detector reads accurately. When we find them, we can always ask them, but in the meantime, we'll have to guess."

Annie started walking back to the hole where Peggy had claimed to find the body. As she started to step down into it, I asked her, "What are you doing?"

"If there was any evidence down here before, Kathleen would have already disturbed it. I want to see if there's anything here that might provide a motive for murder."

I watched my twin sister for a second as she pawed through the dirt before I got down on my hands and knees and started feeling through the weeds around the excavation. Annie noticed what I was doing and asked me, "What are *you* looking for? There's a pile of dirt right there they dug up. If there's anything to find, don't you think it would be somewhere in there?"

I looked over at the red clay soil, mounded up like a tombstone at one end of the hole. "If there had been something there before, surely they would have found it."

"I still think we should check it out," she said.

"I can do that," I said as I stood and moved over the dirt. Grabbing a heavy stick along the way, I used it to probe the soil they'd taken out of the hole, but I didn't find anything. "No luck," I said. "How about you?"

"I can't do much without a shovel," she said. "The soil is pretty dense at this level."

"Then I guess it's a wash," I said as something caught my eye. A beam of light had illuminated something in the grass for just a second, and I bent down to see what it might be.

I'd been hoping for a gold coin, so in that respect, I was disappointed, but what I did find was still interesting, nonetheless.

CHAPTER 7: ANNIE

"WHAT DID YOU FIND, PAT?"

My brother held something up in the light, and I could see it was nothing more exciting than a small button from a jacket. "It's got to be a clue, doesn't it?" he asked me.

"How can you be sure of that? It's hard to know how long it's been here."

"The thread is still attached, Annie," he said as he held it up so I could get a closer look at it. "It hasn't been here that long."

"It still might not mean anything," I said, not wanting my brother to get his hopes up too high. "With all of this activity, it's not hard to believe that someone lost it working."

"Maybe so," Pat said, "but it *could* be significant."

"It might help if we knew whose jacket it matched," I said.

"That's where our detective work comes in," Pat said. "We find the person who lost this button, and then we ask them about what really happened to Bones." He got out his handkerchief and wrapped the button in it, being careful to keep the thread attached.

"Hang on a second," I said as I took out my phone.

"You're not calling Kathleen now, are you?" I asked her. "It's too soon to report this, if you ask me. There might be something else we're missing."

"Take it easy. I'm not calling her. Let me see that button again."

He did as I asked, and once I had a good shot, I took a few photos of it with my phone, trying to get a good image of the thread as well. I wasn't sure how good the color match would be, but at least we'd have some evidence of what we'd found for ourselves once we turned it over to Kathleen.

"Smart thinking, Annie," Pat said.

"Thanks. Now what do we do?"

Pat got down on his hands and knees and looked again at the grass near where he'd discovered the button.

"What's so interesting?" I asked him.

"Come over and look at this for a second, would you?"

Had he found something else? I joined my brother and tried to see what he was pointing to, but I couldn't see a thing out of the ordinary. "What is it? What am I missing?"

"Look at the way the weeds and grass are lying through here," he said.

It took me a second, but then I saw what he was talking about. "Something was dragged through the grass, and fairly recently, too."

"That's what I think," Pat said. "Like a body, perhaps?"

"Bones wasn't that big. How hard would it have been for the killer to throw him over his shoulder and carry him to the van?"

"I'm not so sure it was the weight so much as having a dead body slung over your back. He might not have been dragged because of his weight, but more due to the fact that he was dead. If that was the case, it wouldn't matter if the killer was a man or a woman."

I nodded and tried to get a picture of the disturbed ground as well, but my camera wasn't nearly sophisticated enough to pick up what our naked eyes saw. "It's no good," I said, putting my phone away. "I can't get anything usable."

"But we know that it's here," Pat said.

"Sure, but what can we do with the information?"

"What we always do," I reminded him. "We file it all away in our minds, and when we have enough of the puzzle, we figure out who killed Bones."

"I have a feeling that we're going to need a lot more information than we have right now," he said.

"True, but that shouldn't stop us from trying," I replied. I gestured toward the shallow hole where Bones had been found and the parts of the land that had been excavated, both on my land and on Timothy's acreage. "Killing that young man here is a desecration, as far as I'm concerned, so while I might not know anything about him, and nothing I've heard about him makes me like him even a little bit, I'm still going to find out who killed him. Are you willing to help me do that?"

"I'm here, aren't I?" I asked her.

"Thanks, Pat. I knew I could count on you."

"You shouldn't even have to ask." He cocked an ear and said, "Someone's coming."

"It looks like Kathleen's deputies are finally showing up."

I was wrong, though.

It was someone else entirely who drove down the narrow lane toward us, someone I hadn't been expecting at all.

"Timothy, what are you doing here? I didn't think you were coming home until tomorrow," I said as I greeted him.

"What can I say, I got homesick," he answered after he got out of his gray pickup truck and slammed the door. There was a new bumper sticker he'd added to the others already there: *Lumberjacks Do It in the Woods*. Timothy was a tall, handsome man, and I felt a little flutter every time I saw him. We'd been friends forever, but when he'd asked me out on a date, it had still surprised me. Boy, was I ever glad that I'd said yes. I had been a big fan of the man before as a pal, but his stock had instantly rocketed skyward as a boyfriend. "I wanted to check this spot out for my cabin after learning everything I did in class. What are you guys doing out here?" he asked as he glanced at the holes in his land. "Were you looking for something in particular out here?"

"Timothy, we didn't do any of this," I stammered.

He offered me a gentle smile before he spoke. "I'm willing to take your word for it, but if you two didn't, then who did, and more importantly, why?" Timothy kicked at a clod of dirt near the spot where Peggy had claimed that she'd found Bones's body and sent it into the hole.

"Sorry, but you can't do that," Pat said.

"Why on earth not? It's my land, isn't it?"

"It is, but this area just might be an active crime scene," I replied.

"What! A crime scene? What happened?"

"We think someone was murdered here earlier today," Pat explained.

"You *think*? Don't you know for sure one way or the other?"

"It's complicated," I said.

"Well, I've got time. Let's hear it."

Pat and I barely got through our explanation before Kathleen's deputies finally showed up. One of them asked us to leave, and I nodded to Pat. "We'll see you later, Timothy," I told him as my brother and I headed off into the woods to my place.

"You obviously don't have a car with you. Would you both like a ride somewhere?"

"Why not?" I asked. I'd intended on going back home and waiting for Kathleen to chauffer us back to my car, but this was even better. "We'll take a ride, right, Pat?"

"I'm good with not trudging through the woods," he said. "Let's go."

We were nearly to Timothy's truck when I asked Pat softly, "What about the button? Are you going to show it to one of the deputies?"

"Don't worry. I'll wait and give it directly to Kathleen," he said.

"What button?" Timothy wanted to know.

"I'll tell you later," I replied. "Keep your voice down."

"Fine, but I want it duly noted how gracious I'm being about all of this."

I kissed his cheek. "It is noted."

"That's all I'm asking," he said with a grin. "Now let's get out of here, shall we?"

"Okay, but I need to mention something first," I said as I walked over to one of the deputies. "Hank, you might want to get a little video over here."

"What did you spot, Annie?"

"See how the grass is lying down along here?" I pointed out.

"No, I don't see…wait a second. There it is. Good spot."

"Thank you."

"Is there anything else I might be missing?" he asked me.

I wanted to tell him right then and there, but I still thought it was a better idea to tell Kathleen directly. "We're good."

"Thanks again."

After I rejoined Pat and Timothy, I asked, "We're grateful for the ride and all, but do you have to drop us off right away?"

"No, I'm free for the rest of the day," he said. "I wasn't planning on coming back this early, so no one expects to see me at the office until tomorrow. What did you have in mind?"

"If you two would like to be alone, you can drop me off anywhere along the main road," Pat said. "I don't want to be a third wheel."

"You're coming with us," I said.

"Why are you suddenly so insistent about us having a chaperone?" Timothy asked me with a grin.

"Because we're not going out, at least not on a date. I have something else in mind for us."

"I'm intrigued. What are we going to do?"

"We're going to go looking for a camper van," I answered.

CHAPTER 8: PAT

Annie's suggestion was a good one, and I was glad that Timothy was willing to go along with it. To my surprise, we didn't have far to look.

We found the van parked in the sheriff's headquarters parking lot.

"Wow, Kathleen must be even better than I thought," I said.

"Do you think she's arrested the killer already?" Annie asked. Did my twin sister actually sound a little disappointed by the prospect?

"Hang on. From what you two have told me, we still don't know for sure if anyone's even dead," Timothy added.

"You weren't there when Peggy came to us and we saw the blood all over her. She was pretty convincing that something bad had happened to Bones."

"I'm not saying that she didn't believe it herself, but she could have been wrong. I know for a fact that a head wound can be pretty minor, but it's bloody as can be. One of the men in my class this week hit his head on the corner of a beam, and it bled like crazy before he was able to get it stopped. There's no sense in jumping to conclusions until we have more information, so let's go in and see what we can find out," Timothy said.

"What makes you think Kathleen's going to tell us anything?" I asked him.

Timothy looked surprised by my question. "She's your big sister. Why wouldn't she share what she's uncovered?"

Annie shrugged. "You'd be surprised."

"It's still worth a shot asking her, isn't it?" Timothy asked as he parked the truck next to the van.

"Why not?" I asked. "Like you said, we have nothing to lose."

When the three of us walked into the station, it was time for our next surprise. Instead of being interrogated by Kathleen, three of the college students were just sitting there alone in the waiting area. Henry, Marty, and Gretchen all looked pretty upset, but we didn't know yet what it was all about.

Henry spotted me immediately and stood up. "Finally, a friendly face in this town. Pat, can you help us?"

"I'll do what I can," I said. "What's going on?"

"Life was fine after we had lunch at the Iron, and we were all working in different sections of our dig when things started to fall apart. We can't find Peggy or Bones, and to make matters worse, we had to abandon our site."

Ignoring the first part of his statement, I asked, "Why did you have to leave?"

"The guy who owned the property showed up and threw us off his land," Henry said with a shrug. "We went by the Iron, but you were already closed for the day, so the only other thing we could think of doing was coming here."

Timothy took a step forward. "What did this guy who claimed to own the land look like?" Since he was the rightful owner, I understood him being upset about being impersonated.

Henry scratched his chin before he spoke. "He was pretty fit for his age, probably somewhere in his sixties if I had to guess, and he had a streak of gray running through his hair that made him look kind of like a skunk."

The description was on the nose, and I had no trouble recognizing who he was talking about. It was Carter Hayes, retired from his civil service job for years. These days, he mostly spent his time being a thorn in everyone else's side. He was one of the greediest, cheapest, and most miserly men I'd ever known. I had no problem believing that Carter would throw the college kids off of land he didn't even own.

Timothy spoke up. "Well, for your information, it's my land, and while I wasn't the one who threw you off, Carter did me a favor. What were you thinking, digging all of those holes on somebody else's property without getting permission first?"

"Let's not get off the main subject," I said. I understood Timothy's frustration, but we had something more important to worry about at the moment. "Henry, we need to talk about Bones."

"Do you know where he is?" Gretchen asked. "Is he somewhere with Peggy? It's not like the two of them to just run off like that."

"I thought Peggy left to go get supplies," Annie said.

"Have you seen her? You must have if you know that. Where is she?"

"She's at the hospital," Annie replied.

Henry's face lost its color. "What happened to her? Is she okay?"

"She's going to be fine," I reassured him. "She told us that she left to get supplies for dinner, but when she got back, most of you were gone."

"What do you mean, most of us?" Marty asked. "Did she at least find Bones? And if she's okay, then why is she in the hospital?"

"Finding Bones's body at the dig site was too much for her," Annie said. I'd been half expecting her to say something inflammatory, and I watched everyone closely to see if any of them showed a single sign of recognition, but the truth was that they *all* looked stunned by the news.

"He's dead?" Gretchen asked. "He can't be!"

"As a matter of fact, we don't know that just yet," I said.

Henry held up his hands. "Hang on a second. You just told us that she found his body. That implies that he is dead, doesn't it?"

"The key is that Peggy *told* us that's what happened, but so far, no one else has seen the body," I answered.

"Then let's go to the site and look for him," Gretchen insisted as she headed for the door.

"I can save you all a trip. We've already been there," Annie explained softly. "There was no sign that anything had happened there at all."

"If Peggy said she saw it, then that's what happened. She wouldn't lie about something like that." Henry was pretty emphatic about that, and I wondered if they were more than just friends.

"Would you mind if we looked in the back of the van while you're waiting on the sheriff?" I asked them.

"Why? What does that have to do with anything?" Marty insisted on knowing.

"I'm not sure, but if you don't have anything to hide, why would you care if we had a look?" Annie asked him.

"Get a warrant, and then you can look all you like," Marty said sharply.

Henry shook his head. "Don't be stupid, Marty." He turned to me and said, "Of course you can look. In fact, let's all go to the parking lot right now together. At this point, I'm not even sure the sheriff is coming back. They told us to be patient, but I'm not sure that we have any left."

I neglected to tell any of them that the sheriff was our sister, and evidently Annie didn't feel the need to share that information, either. "No worries on that count. If she does come in, we'll see her out there."

We got to the van, and Henry unlocked every door to it and swung them all wide open. "Help yourself."

"I still don't like this, on principle, if nothing else," Marty said.

"Henry's right, Marty. We don't have anything to hide," Gretchen reassured him.

It was pretty clear that there wasn't a body in the van at the moment, and it would take a trained forensics team to say whether there'd been any blood spilled in the back. After a quick examination, I said, "You can lock it back up. Thanks."

As Henry did as I suggested, Marty asked, "Just out of curiosity, what exactly were you looking for?"

"Does it matter?" Annie asked. "It wasn't there."

A look of realization spread over Gretchen's face. "You thought we were hiding Bones's body in the van, weren't you?"

"The thought crossed our minds," I said.

Henry looked upset by the suggestion. "We aren't killers, Pat. We want to know what happened to him more than you do. Why are you so interested, anyway?"

"Peggy came to us this afternoon with blood all over her hands and face. As far as we're concerned, that makes it our business."

"I need to see her to be sure that she's okay," Henry said as he reopened the driver's door of the van. "Where exactly is this hospital?"

Kathleen drove up at that moment, and after spotting the van, she pulled her squad car behind it, effectively pinning it in place.

After our sister got out, she asked me, "What's going on here?"

Before I could answer, Henry said, "We came here to report that two of our friends are missing."

"These are the college kids I told you about," I told her.

"Let's all go inside and talk about this," Kathleen said.

"You can't just arrest us," Marty protested. "We know our rights. We haven't done anything."

Kathleen stood inches from him. "Who said anything about arresting you? That's interesting that you'd jump to that conclusion. Do you have a guilty conscience, maybe?"

"I couldn't, because I haven't done anything to feel guilty about," Marty said, though he shrank back a little as he said it. Kathleen could be pretty intimidating when she chose to be.

"Good. Then like I said, let's go in and talk about it," our sister said.

The three students agreed, and the three of us naturally followed them all inside. Kathleen noticed our behavior, but she didn't comment on it directly. "Since there are so many of us, let's go into the main interrogation room, okay?"

"Why, are you going to interrogate us?" Gretchen asked, clearly upset by the prospect.

"Let's call it the conference room instead if that makes you feel any better," Kathleen answered, doing her best to put them all at ease.

Annie, Timothy, and I followed them as well, but Kathleen stopped us as the students entered the largest room in the precinct. "I'll be right with you," she told them, and then she closed the door. Turning to us, she said, "I'm truly sorry, but I can't allow any of you inside during an official interrogation."

"I thought it was just a conference?" I asked her with a grin.

She didn't return it. "We both know better. Something's going on, and I aim to find out exactly what it is."

"So then, you believe Peggy?" Annie asked her.

"Unless she's completely delusional, something happened out at your land, Timothy. If this kid everyone keeps calling Bones isn't dead, he's in bad need of a doctor."

"What about your theory that she was on some kind of drugs?" Annie asked her.

"They did a blood test. She's clean. That gives her story about Bones a little more credibility than it had before." She gestured toward the closed interrogation room door. "I'm going to get it out of them, one way or another."

"They all claimed to be just as surprised about the disappearance as we were," I said.

Kathleen looked hard at me for a moment before speaking. "Pat, don't think that I don't appreciate you bringing these kids to me, but that's where it ends. I have to handle this myself."

"I understand," I said. "For what it's worth, the body isn't in the van at this moment, not that it wasn't necessarily there earlier."

"You searched their van? You can't do that!"

I'd clearly struck a nerve, and I was about to defend myself when Annie did it for me. "We asked them nicely if they'd mind if we looked around, and they opened all of the doors for us willingly. There was no duress or threat, implied or otherwise, Kathleen."

That seemed to calm her down a little. "Maybe not, but I still don't like it."

"Then I'm not sure how you're going to feel about this," I said as I brought out the button and thread that I'd found near where Peggy had claimed she'd found the body. "This was in the grass."

"And you just picked it up?" she asked as she took it from me. "What were you thinking, Patrick?"

I hated when she used my given name, and it made me a little agitated. "I was thinking that if I left it where it was, there was a chance that your team would miss it altogether."

"Tell her about the drag marks," Annie suggested.

"What are you two talking about?"

"We saw evidence in the grass and weeds that something heavy had been dragged from that dig site," I said. "I tried to get a photo of it, but it didn't turn out. Believe me, it was there, though."

"Fine," Kathleen said with a resigned air. "I'll tell my people to look for it. We have a little better equipment than a camera phone."

"I already did. Kathleen, if I hadn't said anything about it, the grass could have bounced back by the time they looked for it if I hadn't mentioned it to Hank," I said. "Anyway, I just thought you should know."

"I appreciate it." She hesitated, and then she added, "I'm sorry I snapped at you both earlier. This vanishing body is driving me crazy. Whether Bones is dead or not, *something* happened out there."

"Good luck figuring it out," Annie said.

"Thanks." She looked at Timothy and added, "I'm sure your first reaction is to go out there and fill in every last one of those holes, but resist the temptation. I'm having the entire area cordoned off, so until you hear otherwise from me, that part of your land is off limits. Understand?"

"I hear you loud and clear," Timothy answered, but it was clear he wasn't happy about it.

"Now, if you all will excuse me, I have work to do," Kathleen said as she disappeared into the interrogation room.

I would have given anything to be a fly on the wall in there, but it wasn't going to happen.

For now, we were out of the loop, whether we liked it or not.

CHAPTER 9: ANNIE

"I'M GLAD YOU MADE IT back a day early," I told Timothy as he, Pat, and I walked out of the police station. "I missed you." I kissed him lightly, or at least I tried to, but he pulled away a little at the last second. Was he shy about me bussing him with Pat there?

"Me, too," he said.

I glanced over at Pat to see if he'd been watching us, but he was careful to be looking elsewhere when I did.

"Would you like me to make you something good for dinner tonight?" I offered, trying my best not to sound peeved about the refusal. "We just got a great deal on pork roast, and I've been dreaming about ways of making it in my cast iron Dutch oven."

"As tempting at that sounds, what I really need this evening is sleep. Do you mind too much if I take a rain check, Annie? That course was exhausting. I'm going to go home and collapse."

"I totally get that," I said, trying to hide my disappointment again.

"If you're sure, then as soon as I drop you two off at the Iron, I'm heading home."

"No need to even do that," I said, fighting to keep my voice light. "Pull over. We can walk from here."

Timothy's face clouded a little. "Come on, there's no need to be that way. I have time to at least take you back to your vehicles."

"Don't be silly. We're fine, aren't we, Pat?"

My twin brother knew better than to argue with me at that moment if I'd offered to walk a hundred miles instead of one. "It's true. I need to stretch my legs a little." After Timothy pulled the truck over, Pat got out and said, "Annie, if it's all the same to you, I'm going to pop into the auto supply store. I need to pick up new windshield wipers. See you around, Timothy. Thanks for the lift."

"You're welcome," Timothy said to his retreating back. I had no idea if my brother needed new wipers or not, but I couldn't blame him for getting away from us as quickly as he could manage it. It was pretty obvious that he wasn't sure if there was about to be a scene, and at the very least, he wanted to give us some privacy. If it had been him and Jenna, I would like to think that I would have done the same thing for him.

"Annie, I swear I don't mean anything by turning down your generous offer to feed me. If it means that much to you, I'd be happy to have dinner with you."

"Thanks, but I'd never forgive myself for depriving you of your rest. I'll see you later."

Now that my brother was gone, it was clear that my boyfriend was ready for that kiss, but I wasn't in any mood to give him one now. Even as I forced a smile and walked away from the truck, I was beating myself for acting like a petulant little girl. Why did I do that sometimes? Just when I thought I was finally growing up, I'd have a brief relapse of my adolescence.

I glanced backward as I walked into the automotive parts store and saw Timothy still watching me with a deep frown. Oh, well. I'd make it up to him later, but for now, I had no choice but to play it out until the end.

Pat looked me over carefully when I joined him inside the store. "What is it?" I asked him. "What are you looking for?"

"Well, I don't *see* any blood," he said with the hint of a smile.

I could stay in my little snit, or I could smile and accept his comment for what it was: a way to break the mood and make me smile. I was proud when I realized that it would be the latter, not the former. That still didn't make me a grownup, but at least I felt a little better about myself. "I overreacted back there, didn't I?"

"Are you kidding? I thought you used great restraint, Annie."

"Pat, this is no time to make fun of me."

"I'm not. I swear, I couldn't believe he had the nerve to turn down your invitation. Even if your cooking wasn't suitable for stray dogs, which everyone who has ever tasted knows that's far from the case, that was an invitation he should have accepted. I'm not the greatest guy in the world when it comes to reading a woman's signals, but man, he makes me look downright smooth sometimes."

"Well, I wouldn't go that far," I said with a smile.

"For what it's worth, I'd still be honored to have dinner with you. Tell you what. Why don't we go back to the Iron, and I'll make something for you for a change?"

"As much as I appreciate the gesture, would it be okay with you if I cooked instead?" I loved my brother dearly, but I was in no hurry to sample his food again any time soon.

"It would be a great deal more than okay, as far as I'm concerned," he said with a grin. "Can we still have that pork roast you were talking about? Ever since you mentioned it, I've been trying not to drool on my chin."

"Why not?" I asked with a laugh.

He started to walk out of the store when I stopped him. "What about your wiper blades?"

"What? Oh. I don't know the right size I need. I'll have to come back when I'm driving."

I looked at him skeptically, but I decided not to push it. After all, it wouldn't be fair to point out that his excuse to leave me alone to deal with Timothy had been for my benefit and not his.

It was a pleasant late afternoon, and I enjoyed the walk back to the Iron with my brother. Thankfully no one was waiting for us when we got there, but I didn't like the look of that bloody handprint that was still on the door. The blood had darkened somewhat and now looked crimson. "Pat, if you'll clean that up with some ammonia window cleaner, I'll get things started for our supper."

"Tell you what. Let me watch you prepare the pork roast, and then I'll clean the window when you put it in the oven. Is that a deal?"

"Since when did you take so much interest in my cooking?"

"What if you're gone sometime and I have to fend for myself or, worse yet, run the grill in your place?" he asked me.

"Me? Where would I go?" I asked him.

"Who knows? You might want to take a trip someday."

"Not alone I won't, and the prospect of going with anyone else seems farfetched at the moment," I answered.

"Do you mind an audience while you cook?" he asked again. "If you don't want me hovering around, I understand completely."

"Don't be silly. You're more than welcome to watch."

We walked inside together, and I noticed that Pat was careful to lock the door behind us. Flipping on a few lights, we made our way back to the grill. I took out one of my favorite Dutch ovens and put it on the counter. Preheating the oven to 325 degrees F, I took out a two-pound roast and put it on one of my cutting boards reserved for meat only. Taking a sharp knife, I cut diagonal diamonds on the fat side, piercing the thin layer with two-inch-deep cuts about the same distance from each other. Taking some of the sauce I loved, I rubbed it into the top, being sure to get sauce into the crevasses I'd created. "Normally I'd let this marinate for four or five hours, but I think we'll be fine if we go ahead and pop it straight into the oven. Besides, you don't want to wait until midnight to eat, do you?"

"Not with our schedule set for getting up bright and early tomorrow," Pat said from a barstool across from where I was working.

"I didn't think so," I answered with a smile. Taking out another knife and a clean cutting board, I prepped an onion, slicing it horizontally to make rings from it, peeled and chopped large chunks of carrots, and then quartered a few medium-sized potatoes. "Does that look like enough vegetables for you?" I asked him.

"Aren't you having any?" he asked me with a grin.

I added another potato, a few more carrots, and one more onion, and then I spread them out on the bottom of the Dutch oven. After that, I poured in about a cup of beef broth and then added the pork roast last.

"Why beef broth for cooking pork?" Pat asked.

"Just about any liquid will do," I said. "There's something about the beef broth as it steams that I like, though I've used water in the past, wine, and even some hard cider once."

"How was that?" he asked me.

"Not good enough to justify giving up the hard cider," I told him with a grin as I covered the lid. The oven reached its temperature, and I put the cast iron pot inside and then set my timer for an hour and forty-five minutes.

Pat must have seen the setting. "Do we really have to wait that long?"

"Well, we might be able to get away with just an hour, but I don't like to take any chances with pork. I know the government has come out saying that an internal temperature of 145 degrees F is enough, but I like mine to be at least 160. If you're feeling lucky, though, we can always roll the dice."

"No, your way sounds fine to me," he said. "Is that all there is to it?"

"Pat, I don't make magic back here. Most of the work is done by the oven and the cast iron."

"I don't know. That seemed pretty labor intensive to me."

"Trust me, it's not. This is one of the easiest meals I make."

"Then why don't you serve it more often?" he asked me.

"Mostly because of the high price of those roasts. If I could get a bargain like I did on these, I'd make this all the time. Now, what do we do in the meantime?"

"I've got a window to clean, remember?" he asked with a grin.

"I don't mind doing it, if you'd rather not."

"No thanks. A deal is a deal. You cooked, so the least I can do is clean the window."

"I'll at least keep you company," I said.

We walked out together, and Pat had the glass shining again in no time. "There. It looks as good as new, doesn't it? That was easy enough. It still leaves us with an hour and a half to kill, though," he said.

"Maybe we should come up with a different expression, given the circumstances."

"What circumstances are those, exactly? We don't have a body, and the only eyewitness's account is a bit shaky, and that's putting it lightly. If she really saw Bones in that hole, then what happened to him? Did someone drag him away, or did he crawl?" Pat asked.

"Did the way that grass and those weeds were bent look as though he could have crawled away under his own power?" I asked him.

"I don't know. All I can say for sure is that he was nowhere around that dig site when we checked it out."

"I wonder if Kathleen's deputies found anything that we missed," I said.

Pat frowned before he spoke. "We both know that we won't hear a word about it, even if they did. Unless."

"Unless what?"

"Why don't we invite Kathleen to join us for dinner?" he suggested.

"There's enough to share, isn't there?"

"We could feed six people, if we had to, based on how many vegetables I put in that pot," I conceded.

"You're right. That gives me an even better idea. We could invite her, and the three college kids, too. After all, they have to eat something, don't they?"

"Pat, do you honestly believe that Kathleen is going to fall for that?"

"The only way to find out is to ask her," he said with his most impish grin.

Why not? What could it hurt to at least make the offer? If she declined, then at least we'd tried to do something constructive. And if she said yes, we might end up getting more out of those students than anyone could expect. "There's just one problem with your idea," I told him.

"What's that?"

"If we succeed, there won't be any seconds, let alone leftovers."

Pat pretended to ponder that for a full ten seconds before he finally shrugged. "If it helps our investigation, then it's a sacrifice I'm willing to make."

"Wow, now I know that you're serious," I told him as I picked up my cellphone and made the call.

To my surprise, Kathleen agreed to the plan almost immediately, whether it was because of what I was offering or because it gave her an opportunity to extend her examination of these kids.

Either way, it looked as though Pat and I hadn't been completely cut out of her investigation after all, and Timothy's refusal to have dinner with me had made that possible in the first place. If I was being mature about it, I'd thank him someday.

Just not today.

CHAPTER 10: PAT

"WE NEED TO COME UP with a plan before everyone gets here," I told Annie after she got off the phone with our older sister.

"I thought that after everyone got here, we'd eat, and then we'd have ourselves a nice little chat," she said.

"Don't you think we need to come up with something better than that?"

"Pat, Kathleen has been grilling them for over an hour. Do you really think we should hit them with more questions of our own? Not only will it possibly infuriate our big sister, but the kids are going to resent it as well. On the other hand, if we keep it loose and unrehearsed, we might just be able to learn something new."

"You're right," I said.

"That's what I like I about you. You're not afraid to admit when you're wrong."

"I never said that I was wrong," I corrected her.

"Wasn't it implied? Anyway, we have a little time to kill before everyone gets here. Should we make dessert, too?"

"Do you have time to make a pineapple upside down cake?" I asked her. It was my favorite dessert in the world, and not just because Annie used a cast iron skillet to bake it in. I loved just about everything about it, including the warm pineapple slices and maraschino cherries on top.

"There should be if I get busy on it right away," she said.

As Annie started assembling the ingredients, I asked her, "Should I call the hospital and see if Peggy is still there, or should we just wait and ask Kathleen about her when she gets here?"

"I don't know. It might be awkward to ask with her friends there. Why don't you make the call, and I'll finish this up?"

"Sounds like a good division of labor to me," I said with a grin. "I'll trade a phone call for some of your pineapple upside down cake any day of the week."

I came back into the Iron ten minutes later after going out onto the front porch to make my call. Sometimes I got better reception out there, but this evening it had been a little sketchy even there. The cell phone industry liked to claim that there was coverage everywhere civilization ruled, but there were times when I couldn't even get a signal upstairs in my bedroom. Oddly enough, there were other instances when I had as many as two bars on my phone. I didn't understand it, and no one I'd ever asked had been able to explain it to my satisfaction.

"Did you have any luck?" she asked me.

"They're keeping her overnight," I said.

"Why? Was she hurt after all, or is she really in shock?"

"That I couldn't find out," I answered with a shrug. "But if you ask me, I've got a hunch our big sister has something to do with it. I'm sure she doesn't want her only witness to what might have been a murder disappearing on her."

"Would she really do something like that?"

"I'm sure she believes she's helping Peggy at the same time, but don't kid yourself. Right now, that girl is the only one who believes without hesitation that Bones is really dead."

"Well, I've got to say, if it's a practical joke, it's in pretty horrific taste," Annie said.

"I didn't mean it that way. I'm just wondering if he was unconscious when Peggy found him, but soon after she left, he managed to get away from the site altogether."

"Why hasn't he asked anyone for help if that's what happened?" she asked me.

"Well, someone did just try to kill him, and they failed through no fault of their own, apparently. Wouldn't that make you reluctant to show yourself if it were you?"

"I suppose so," she said. "Maybe I should run home and have a look around before everyone gets here."

I sniffed the air, and I could tell that the roast, as well as the cake, was close to being ready to take out of the oven. "Is that really a very good idea?"

"You can handle things here. Just take everything out when it's ready," she said.

"Why the sudden urge to go home?" I asked her.

"What if Bones woke up and somehow managed to stumble to the nearest house? Where would he go?"

"Your place," I said. I glanced at my watch. "Let's roll. We've got twenty-five minutes before Kathleen shows up. How much time is left on the oven timer?"

"Everything should be finished in around ten minutes."

"Then we wait together and pull everything out of the oven, and then we rush over to your place," I said.

"Pat, it's not going to work. We don't have time to get there and back. Just let me go now."

"Annie, it's not going to happen. You're not going to your place without an escort."

"Then I suppose you can go, too, but I don't know why you're so afraid to do a simple task here."

"Sis, we both know that timing on when something is done is highly subjective, especially with cast iron. You've had a lot more practice with it than I have. But that's not the real reason. Neither one of us needs to go someplace that secluded alone. If Bones really does need help, then he's going to need more than we can give him. We should just call Kathleen, tell her what we're thinking, and then let her check it out herself."

"Why so timid all of a sudden, Pat?" she asked me. "You aren't losing your nerve, are you?"

"You bet I am," I said without hesitation. "That's the best way to stay alive, as far as I'm concerned."

Annie hesitated for a full five seconds before she spoke again. "What if he's at my cabin, and he's gravely injured? Any delay may cost him his life. Do you honestly want that hanging over your head for the rest of your life while we try to get ahold of our big sister?"

"That's why I want to tell Kathleen," I said. "As a matter of fact, I think we should call her now."

"Go on," Annie said, "but don't go outside, okay? I'd like to at least hear your end of the conversation when you make the call. Besides, I bet I get better reception in here than you do out on the porch."

"It wouldn't take much," I said as I dialed Kathleen's number.

"We're on our way, Pat, so don't you dare cancel on me at the last minute," our older sister said.

"We wouldn't think of it," I said. "Annie and I have been talking, and there's something we wanted to ask you."

"I can't really talk right now," she said.

"Are you still with the kids? How's that going?"

"Sure, later is fine," Kathleen said.

"So, you don't want to talk about it in their presence, is that it?"

"Absolutely," she said. "Was that all?"

"No. We think you should send someone over to Annie's cabin immediately. What if Bones woke up, stumbled through the woods, and made it to her place? He might be in trouble."

"Yes, we did that already," Kathleen said. "There was no sign of any cat in the tree. It's probably Mrs. Hickman's overactive imagination again. If that's all, I really do have to go. I'm on my way to dinner with friends."

"Got it. See you soon."

I hung up and breathed a sigh of relief.

"What did she say?" Annie asked me.

"They already left, but she managed to let me know that she checked your place out earlier, and it was all clear."

"Did she say that in so many words?"

"No, she had to speak in code, since she wasn't alone. She said that there was no sign of a cat in the tree, so Bones wasn't there when her people checked your place out earlier."

Annie frowned at me. "That's quite a leap going from looking for Bones to not seeing a treed cat, wouldn't you say?"

"You had to hear both sides of the conversation to fully understand," I said. "She didn't want to tip the kids off about what we were talking about. It made perfect sense to me."

"Is that why Kathleen gets so frustrated with us sometimes? I swear, it's like you two were speaking in some kind of code that I wasn't aware of."

"The only secret language I know is the one we made up as kids," I said with a smile.

"Looking back on it, we must have driven everyone around us crazy back then."

"What makes you think that stopped when we grew up?" I asked her.

Annie pulled out the Dutch oven with our pork roast and lifted the lid to peek inside. The aromas were nearly magical, and I was beginning to regret inviting anyone else. Still, it was for a good cause, so I decided to keep my disappointment to myself. Next, the pineapple upside down cake came out, and I immediately started having regrets again. The sacrifices I was willing to make in order to uncover the truth could be quite painful at times.

I heard a car pull up out front, and when I walked to the front of the store, I saw Kathleen get out of her squad car, along with the three kids she'd been interrogating. No one looked particularly happy about being there, so I knew that so far, things hadn't gone that well.

Maybe Annie's food and my company would make things better, but even if they didn't, at least we'd all get to eat a delicious meal and dessert, too.

"Hey, Pat. Hi, Annie. Thanks for feeding us," Henry said solemnly. The young man was quite a bit more subdued than he'd been earlier that day when we'd first met. Had it really just been that afternoon that all of our paths had crossed for the first time?

"It's our pleasure. We're just sorry about everything that's been happening today," I said.

"Tell me about it," Gretchen said. "Hey."

"Hello."

Marty just scowled at us all, including the college kids he'd come to Maple Crest with. As a matter of fact, he looked as though he'd rather be anywhere else at the moment than at the Iron, and I didn't blame him one bit. They'd come in search of treasure and wealth, and all they'd managed to dig up was tragedy, if Peggy's story was to be believed.

"I hope you're all hungry," Annie said as Kathleen came in last, carefully locking the door behind her. "We've got pork roast and pineapple upside down cake for dinner and dessert."

Gretchen frowned. "I'm sorry, but I can't stand pork," she said glumly. "Oh well. At least I can have some cake, unless there's pork in that, too."

"Nonsense. I can whip something else up for you. You're not a vegetarian, are you?"

"No, I just don't like pork," she repeated.

"How about an omelet?" Annie offered.

"Or I could make you one of my special egg and cheese sandwiches," I volunteered. "While Annie's the pro at just about everything else in the cooking world, I'm the king of egg sandwiches around here."

"That sounds nice," Gretchen said as she smiled at me, "but only if it's not too much trouble."

"It's no problem at all," I said as Marty's scowl turned particularly malevolent when he turned to me. It appeared that he had a bit of a crush on Gretchen, and he wasn't all that pleased that another man had her attention, even if for only a moment. I just shrugged as I took my place behind the counter while Annie joined the others. She set all of the places as I grated some cheese and started two eggs in a pan. Popping the bread down in the toaster, I worked with practiced ease, since this was my preferred meal most evenings Annie didn't volunteer to feed me. Was this how it felt for her, mistress of her domain as she prepared everyone's food? It was nice, I had to admit, not that I ever had any interest in changing places with her on more than an occasional basis. Annie was just serving the others as I finished Gretchen's sandwich. Her thanks were out of proportion for what I offered her, which managed to make Marty a little angrier still, something I hadn't been at all sure would be possible earlier.

As we ate, there was very little conversation besides a polite request for salt or pepper or a refill of sweet tea. I'd been hoping for an open discussion, but we might as well have been eating under vows of silence. Kathleen tried to ask them all a few questions, but her inquiries were met with utter quiet, so eventually she stopped even trying.

After we all finished dessert, which was just as amazing as the pork roast had been, Kathleen said, "That was truly outstanding. I suppose we'd better get back to the station, though."

"Do we honestly have to go back there tonight?" Henry asked. "We're exhausted. It would be great if we could get our camping equipment out of the van and set up at the park, or somewhere else that's out of the way."

"There's no camping allowed there," Kathleen said, "and besides, we're still going through all of your things."

"Where are we supposed to sleep, then?" Marty asked. "We can't afford a motel room, even a cheap one. Bones is the money in this operation. The rest of us are just a bunch of broke students."

"I suppose you could always sleep at the jail," Kathleen said. "It's not much, but I can offer you cots and blankets."

I had a sudden thought. Without even consulting with Annie, I suggested, "Nonsense. They can stay here tonight with me."

Annie and Kathleen stared at me with the exact same expression of disbelief in their eyes, as though I'd just lost my mind. I knew that I'd just invited one potential murderer into my business and my home, but I hadn't been able to stop myself.

"Where are we supposed to sleep, on the floor?" Marty asked.

"Hey, don't be so ungrateful," Henry replied, perking up from the meal he'd just eaten. "I'll happily take a spot on the floor, if that's all you've got."

"Nonsense," Annie said, getting into the spirit of things. "We have air mattresses and sleeping bags. You can all sleep in the storeroom."

"Do you really trust us down here with all of your stuff?" Gretchen asked.

"It's not like we won't be nearby," Annie said. "Pat and I just will be upstairs."

"You two *live* together, too?" Gretchen asked as she frowned a little upon hearing the news. "I don't know how you keep from killing each other. Sorry. That was a poor choice of words."

"No, but sometimes when I don't want to go back to the cabin, I crash on Pat's couch. Besides, if I hang around tonight, I'll be able to make breakfast for everyone tomorrow morning." She turned to Kathleen. "What do you say? Will that work for you?"

"It will be fine, but I need you all in my office at eight tomorrow morning, and not a minute late. Is that understood?"

"Completely," Henry said. "Right, guys?"

"I guess," Marty said.

"It sounds like fun," Gretchen added.

"Then I'll see you in the morning," Kathleen said, and then she turned to me. "May I have a word with you out on the porch, Pat?"

I recognized that look on her face. I was about to get a lecture for a class I hadn't signed up for. Annie stepped in. "I'll get you all set up in the back while they are chatting. It's not much, but at least there's a bathroom and space to spread out."

The three students followed her into the back room as I left the Iron, if only for a few moments, with Kathleen.

Before she could start in on me, I said, "Save the lecture, Sis. I know what I'm doing."

"Really? That seems highly unlikely to me at the moment. What were you thinking, Patrick?"

There was my full first name again. "I doubt spending the night in a jail cell is going to loosen any tongues. Having them here tonight, we might be able to get something out of them. Have *you* had any luck so far?"

"No," she admitted reluctantly. "Everybody keeps pleading ignorance except Peggy."

"You're holding her at the hospital overnight, aren't you?" I asked.

"How did you know that?"

"I called and asked them," I admitted. "Don't worry. We'll be fine."

"I hope so, but just in case, your door upstairs has a deadbolt lock on it, doesn't it?"

"You know that it does."

"Use it tonight, okay?"

"Kathleen, why would anyone want to hurt Annie and me?"

"I don't know, but until we get this mess sorted out, keep your eyes open. Tell Annie to do the same, too."

"Will do," I said.

"I still think you're crazy for doing this," she said with a sigh.

"Really? I couldn't tell," I answered with a grin.

"If you do happen to learn anything, call me, and don't give one thought about what time it might be. I doubt I'll sleep a wink as it is."

"You're welcome to join us," I said happily. "You know what they say, the more the merrier." I couldn't figure out why I was smiling, and then I realized that it was because Annie and I were doing something active rather than waiting for something to happen for us to react to.

"Thanks, but I'd rather sleep in my squad car. No offense."

"None taken," I said.

"Don't make me live to regret this, Pat," Kathleen said as she took a step off the porch toward her cruiser.

"I'll do my best," I replied. "See you in the morning."

"I fervently hope so," she answered, which somehow managed to take the smile off my face. I'd known the arrangements I'd proposed had been risky, and I hadn't given my offer much thought before I'd made it.

Maybe Kathleen was right, but it was too late now.

Annie and I were committed.

I just hoped that neither of my sisters had any reason to regret my impulsive offer later.

CHAPTER 11: ANNIE

Gretchen and Henry offered to help clean up, while Marty watched them sullenly. I oversaw the operation and found it a good time to chat with everyone. When Henry reached for the soap, though, I knew that I had to intervene. "No soap on the cast iron."

"Seriously?" he asked. "How do you get it clean?"

"Let me show you," I said as I gently took his place at the sink. Taking my special nylon scrubbing tool, I ran fresh water in the bottom of the Dutch oven and used the pad to gently work any stuck food loose. There was a bit of onion adhering to the bottom, but it came off quickly, and soon I had the pot in perfect shape again.

"Aren't you worried about food contamination?" Gretchen asked me as I dried the pot and lid with paper towels.

"It's essentially a nonstick surface," I told them. "If there's anything stuck to it that I can't get off easily, I boil water in the pot for a few minutes, and that releases everything. The iron is well seasoned, so it works beautifully."

"What does that mean?" Marty asked, interested despite his nature.

"When I get a new skillet or pot, the first thing I do is to strip it down to the bare metal."

"By electrolysis?" Gretchen asked. I'd forgotten that she was the true scientist among the group.

"You can use that method, but I prefer soaking it overnight in a vinegar-and-water mixture," I said. "It's amazing how much rust that process will remove. Once the pan is free of rust and any past seasoning, it's time to start over. Do you all really care about this?"

They all assured me that they did. I grabbed the Dutch oven and showed them. "Let's pretend this hasn't been seasoned at all. After it's down to bare metal, I take some olive oil and pour just a little into the bottom. Before I do that, though, I have to dry it thoroughly."

"I thought you just did that," Henry said.

"I got the surface moisture off, but rust is cast iron's biggest enemy. Don't worry, this won't take long," I said as I put the pot and its lid, separately, back into the oven. After I was sure that it was bone dry, I removed both pieces from the heat and set them aside. "We can get started on seasoning now." I performed each step as I explained it. "After I add a little oil, I take a paper towel or an old cotton cloth, and I rub it into the bottom and sides of the pot until there's no puddling. This takes several coats, because you can't rush the process or you get an oil buildup that can trap food or get rancid all on its own. After that, I put the pot on the stovetop and warm it gently until the oil is soaked up."

"What if it's got legs on it like this one?"

"Then I do it in the oven," I told Henry. "On indoor Dutch ovens like this one, the bottom is flat and the lid is domed, so I can heat the pot on the stovetop when I season the inside. Outdoor models have three legs, and the lid has a lip to hold coals in place, so that needs to be done in the oven or over an open fire. Anyway, you repeat this process, slowly adding oil, heating it, and then wiping away the excess once it's warmed again."

"How do you know when it's finished?" Gretchen asked.

"A true cast iron cook will tell you that it's *never* finished, but there comes a stage when it's ready for the final step. This time I rub the entire pot and lid, inside and out, with another thin coat of oil, and I let it bake at around 350 degrees F for an hour. After that time is up, I take everything out, being careful not to burn myself because the iron retains heat for a long time, carefully rub it down again, and then it's ready to use."

"I don't know. It seems like a lot of work to me," Marty said.

"It might look that way at first, but after you have a well-seasoned skillet or pot, it's a breeze to keep up with. And the flavors are unbelievable."

"Aren't you worried about getting too much iron in your diet?" Gretchen asked me.

"It's true that my levels are slightly elevated, but my doctor isn't too concerned about it, so neither am I. As a matter of fact, he's taken one of my outdoor cooking classes, and now he cooks with cast iron himself. That's enough about me, though. How did the five of you get together?"

"We were recruited," Henry said. "I suppose in a way, this is all my fault."

"You can't blame yourself," Gretchen said, touching his shoulder lightly, something that made Marty's perpetual frown deepen even further. "It wasn't your fault."

"If I hadn't found that journal in the first place, and the map that Jasper Blankenship drew in it, Bones would still be alive, and Peggy wouldn't be in the hospital right now."

"How did you happen to stumble across it in the first place?" Pat asked from off to one side. He'd been so quiet that I'd nearly forgotten that my brother was there.

"I was logging in a box of old papers and journals that someone had donated to the college. Folks do that sometimes rather than just throw them out, something we greatly appreciate. Anyway, I have to add a description to every piece we keep, so I started leafing through Jasper's journal. There was a crudely drawn sketch in it, but there weren't any points of reference to show where it might actually be. Age hadn't been kind to the paper, so it was difficult to make out what it represented. Adding to the confusion was the fact that the location of the X on his map seemed to have been changed a dozen times over the years. Evidently Jasper had a habit of burying his stash of money in one place for a while and then digging it up again and moving it later."

"What I don't understand is why his family didn't use the map to get the money for themselves," I asked.

"We speculate that Jasper not only hid his money, but he stashed his journal away somewhere where it wasn't easy to find, too. The man was clearly paranoid. Reading his journal is a pretty clear indicator of that, not to mention his odd sense of humor."

"Did he say how much he buried?" Pat asked.

"There are hints among the prose, but it was a lot, that much we're sure of. Could this be a wild goose chase? Of course it could be. Jasper might have dug it up himself and spent it without anyone else knowing about it, or someone else could have discovered it between now and then and not told anyone about finding it. Bones was in the library doing some research on something else while I was doing a little digging myself, and we started talking. We'd had a class together a few years ago, not that we were friends exactly. I filed the journal away, after making copies of it for myself, and I kind of forgot about it until he approached me a month later offering to finance an expedition. I suggested we recruit Peggy, and the others built from there."

"We knew each other from our freshman year in the dorm," Gretchen said.

"I had a class with Bones, too," Marty volunteered.

"So, between the five of you, you had a historian, an archeologist, a cartographer, a mining engineer, and the pre-med student who financed the trip. It sounds like he was pretty thorough assembling his group."

"Only the map turned out to be useless," Marty said with a snarl. "I could roughly identify the areas of some of the Xs he'd drawn once we were on the site, but then it became trial and error."

"I'm surprised you didn't have a metal detector with you," Pat asked. We sold a basic model at the Iron, though it was currently out of stock.

"We had one, but something happened to it after the first hour we used it," Marty allowed. "Bones was getting us another one, but in the meantime, we started digging at every X we could find."

"We haven't had much time on the site, though," Gretchen said, "so we still don't have any idea if anything's buried there or not."

"It hardly matters at this point, does it?" Henry asked. "We're down to three people, and we can't even access the land. All I want to do now is head back to school after we collect Peggy."

"Aren't you worried about Bones?" Pat asked him.

"Of course I am, but there's nothing I can do for him now," Henry said. "He's either okay, or he's not, but either way, it's beyond anything I can do for him. You're right, though. We should at least try to find him before we go."

"That begs the question of how reliable Peggy is," I said gently.

Henry didn't like the implication. "She doesn't lie, if that's what you're asking."

"Never?" Marty asked. "She's not a saint, Henry."

"Be very careful, my friend," Henry said to him, showing a cold anger I hadn't seen before.

"Didn't you get the memo? I'm not your friend," Marty said just as icily.

"Boys, behave yourselves," Gretchen said.

The moment of tension passed, and I was about to ask a follow-up question when there was a knock at the front door. The entire town knew we were closed, so who could be knocking this late?

It was our older sister, Kathleen, and she looked pretty grim as Pat and I let her into the Iron.

"What's going on?" I asked her.

"Could you and Pat step outside for a second, Annie?"

I turned to the kids. "We'll just be a minute."

They clearly wanted to know what was going on, but it was just as obvious that our older sister was in no mood to share with them.

Once we were outside, Kathleen said, "We found Bones."

"He's dead, isn't he?" I asked her. There was no other way the discovery would upset her so much.

"Yes."

There it was, short and to the point. Peggy had been right after all.

"Where did you find him?" Pat asked.

Kathleen looked at me a moment before she spoke. "He was at your place, Annie."

I couldn't believe it! "I thought one of your people checked my cabin out."

"She did, but she neglected to look in the pond."

"Bones drowned? After dragging himself through the woods, why would he go into the pond?"

"There's another scenario that's more likely than that," Pat said.

Kathleen nodded. "That's what I'm thinking. Bones never made it out of the woods alive. Someone took his body and threw it into the pond long after he was dead. We'll be able to confirm that theory when they perform his autopsy. If there's no water in his lungs, then he didn't drown."

"Why would anyone move him?" I asked, feeling myself edging up to hysteria. I wasn't sure if I'd ever be able to look at the pond that I'd loved so dearly up until thirty seconds ago again.

"It may have been to remove any evidence that was on the body, or they might have just tried to make it harder to figure out what happened to him," she said.

"Somebody was thinking about muddying the waters, but how did they even know about Annie's place to begin with? That driveway of hers is long and treacherous, and I doubt anyone would venture down it without knowing what they were going to find at the other end," Pat said.

"Who knows? Maybe they didn't even know there was a cabin there, let alone a pond. It may have been a matter of taking the first abandoned-looking road and dumping the body out of sight."

I wasn't sure I liked the reference to my long driveway in to the cabin, but then again, I couldn't exactly dispute it, since it was a pretty accurate description. "What do we do now?"

"I want to tell them," Kathleen explained, "but I want you both to be watching their faces when I do. I have a feeling that two of them are going to be genuinely surprised by the news. We need to spot the one who isn't."

"Because chances are pretty good that's going to turn out to be our killer," I said.

"I'd say the odds would be in favor of it," Kathleen replied.

Before we could go in, Pat said, "Hold up a second. Should we keep the discovery from them? Maybe we'll be able to use it later against them if they think he's still alive."

"It's not going to work," Kathleen said. "I've got a team retrieving the body even as we speak, so the entire town is going to know by morning. We need to use this information while we still have the element of surprise working for us. Be vigilant, you two, okay?"

"We will," Pat and I said almost simultaneously.

"Then let's go tell them the news and see if anyone flinches," Kathleen said.

CHAPTER 12: PAT

"Is there any news about Bones?" Henry asked as my sisters and I walked back into the Iron. Annie was about to say something when I shot her a warning glance. This news was Kathleen's, not ours, and we had no right to share it.

"Bones is dead," she said, and I watched the three students quickly in turn, hoping for some kind of giveaway reaction.

Henry frowned deeply, Marty shook his head, and Gretchen started to cry. She was the first one to speak. "Are you sure? Maybe you made a mistake."

"Someone killed him and dumped him into Annie's pond," Kathleen said severely. "There's no mistaking it."

"Are you sure that he didn't drown accidently?" Henry asked. "Maybe someone hurt him, but his actual death could have been an accident."

"If he sustained the original wounds during a confrontation, legally it doesn't matter," Kathleen said, "but chances are good that he was dead before his body went into the water."

"How can you possibly know that?" Marty asked her.

"Do you really want to know?"

"Please, spare us the details," Gretchen said, crying softly as she spoke. I wasn't even sure she was aware that she was doing it.

"I want to know," Marty said.

"I doubt the coroner will find any fluid in his lungs, based on the severity of his other injuries," Kathleen said. "That means that most likely, he was dead before he hit the water."

"If he didn't drown, then what did kill him?" Henry asked. "Peggy said she found him bloody, but she didn't know much more than that."

"Keep in mind that we just found him, but from our preliminary inspection, it appears that he was struck from behind with a pickaxe."

Gretchen wept softly, and Annie moved to comfort her. Marty wouldn't let it go, though. "At least he didn't know what hit him."

"Marty!" Henry said. "Show some respect."

"He's dead. Bones is way past caring about respect."

"I'm afraid that it wasn't that easy a death," Kathleen said, still watching the three of them closely.

"What do you mean?" Henry asked.

"It's pretty clear that the first blow didn't kill him. It probably wasn't even the second or third."

Gretchen grabbed her mouth. "I'm going to be sick."

"The restroom's back here," Annie said as she led her away.

"Nice, Marty," Henry said. "Are you happy with yourself?"

"Hey, blame the sheriff for her answer. I just asked the question."

"Sorry, but there was no easy way to couch the news," Kathleen said.

I begged to differ, but I wasn't going to do it aloud. My sister had her reasons to use the shock value of the information for her investigation, but that didn't mean that I liked it, let alone agreed with it. Still, she was the sheriff, and I was just a storeowner.

"Does Peggy know you found Bones?" Henry asked.

"Isn't that why she's in the hospital in the first place?" Marty asked. "Finding him was clearly what sent her over the edge."

"We don't know what's going on with her yet," Henry said, and then he turned to Kathleen. "I need to see her."

"Sorry, but she's not allowed to have any visitors right now," Kathleen informed him.

"But I'm her friend," Henry pled. "Can't they make an exception?"

"What good is it going to do her having her suspicions confirmed?" Marty asked. "Let the poor girl rest at least one night without having her worst fears realized."

"Yeah, I can see where you're coming from," Henry said, and then he stared at his fellow student for a moment before adding, "Marty, you don't seem all that upset by the news."

"That's because I figured he was dead from the moment Peggy told everyone that she found him," Marty explained pragmatically.

"Still, somebody died today," Henry insisted.

"Murdered, actually," I added.

"Even worse," Henry responded.

"Come on," Marty said. "Don't pretend that you liked Bones all of a sudden, Henry, just because he's dead now. I saw him putting the moves on Peggy this morning, and what's more, I saw the way you reacted to it. You wanted to kick his tail, and now all of a sudden, you're all broken up because he's dead."

"You hated him because he was rich," Henry accused him. "I watched you bristle every time Bones reminded us that he was financing our dig. It drove you nuts, didn't it?"

Marty just shrugged, but Henry had struck home with his point. I could start to see the method to Kathleen's technique. After she'd dropped her bombshell about finding Bones's body, she sat back and watched her suspects turn on each other.

As if on cue, Gretchen returned, with Annie just behind her. "What did we miss?" my twin sister asked.

"Henry's pretending that he's sorry Bones is dead, even though he wanted to kill him himself this morning because he was jealous," Marty said.

"I was not!" Henry said as he took a step toward Marty, his fists clenched. There was definitely a bit of temper showing, not that he didn't have a reason to be upset.

"What about you, Marty? You didn't like him, either," Henry said.

"Maybe so, but at least he wasn't hitting on my girlfriend, was he?" Marty shot back.

"Peggy is not my girlfriend," Henry said icily.

Did Gretchen look particularly interested as Henry said it? Maybe it was just my imagination, or could she have had a motive herself that we hadn't learned yet? "How did you get along with Bones?" I asked her.

"He was nice enough to me," Gretchen said.

"Tell the truth, Gretchen," Marty said.

After a moment, she wrinkled her nose. "Fine. He was overbearing, and he tried to grope me a couple of times, but he didn't do anything that merited murder."

"I guess you're wrong about that," Kathleen said.

"Why do you say that?" Gretchen asked her.

"He didn't fall on that pickaxe four times by accident," she said calmly.

That tended to end that part of the conversation. When I glanced at Gretchen's jacket, I noticed that a button was missing. The remaining ones looked a great deal like the one I'd uncovered near the crime scene. Had Kathleen spotted it yet? I decided to ask Gretchen about it directly. "What happened to your jacket?"

She looked at the missing button, and then she shrugged it off. "It's been loose for weeks, and I guess it finally came off. I've been meaning to fix it, but I never had the time. Now I'm going to have to find a replacement. What a pain."

It was a logical story, told calmly and believably.

So why didn't I believe her?

Kathleen said, "Given the circumstances, I think it's best if you all come with me after all."

"Are you arresting us?" Marty asked.

"No, I'm renewing my offer of giving you a place to stay tonight. We can take the sleeping bags and air mattresses with us, but it makes more sense if you're at the station in case something else comes up and I need to speak with one of you immediately. If we move the conference table out, you'll have plenty of room to spread out, and there's a bathroom attached to it as well." She turned to me. "Is that okay with you, Pat?"

I wasn't finished with these three, and I had a hunch that Annie wasn't either, but what could I say? There was no legitimate reason to protest the move, especially since we now knew without a doubt that Bones was dead. "That's fine."

Annie nodded, a little reluctantly, and we gathered the bags and mattresses together. Each student carried their own load and thanked us for dinner as they left, even though their praise was halfhearted at best.

"Did you get anything out of them when Kathleen dropped the news about Bones on them?" Annie asked me after they were gone.

"They all reacted, but I don't know any of them well enough to know if any of their responses were out of character for them."

"Where does that leave us, then?" Annie asked.

"I wish I knew. I know you're going to think I'm crazy, but I would still really like you to stay here tonight."

"Why should I do that? The killer, whichever one of them it is, is going to be safely locked away at the police station."

"Maybe so," I said. "But what if they're not?"

"Is there a suspect you haven't told me about?" Annie asked me.

"You know, I hesitate bringing this up, but we've been discounting someone. Up until now we've been treating Peggy as an innocent bystander, but what if she's not? She found the body originally, she had blood all over her, and there's no one who can say whether she killed him herself, moved the body, and then came here to cover up her crime or not."

"I didn't really think of that," Annie admitted, "but while we're throwing out suspects, I think we should look at Carter Hayes, too."

"Carter? Why?"

"He tried to throw those kids off Timothy's land, claiming that it belonged to him."

"That doesn't make him a killer," I said.

"No, but ask yourself a question. What was he doing back there in the first place? What if he got wind of buried riches there, and he wanted whatever was there for himself? You know as well as I do that Carter is the greediest man in four counties. If he got wind that there was money for the taking, what would he stop at to get it?"

"I don't know," I said uneasily. "Should we go talk to him in the morning?"

"We don't have to. He comes in at nine every day to check his mail. I think we should corner him then."

"Okay, but don't do it without me," I told her.

"I wouldn't dream of it," she said, trying not to smile.

"I mean it, Annie. He could be dangerous."

"Everyone we run into these days is potentially a killer," she said. "It's kind of hard at this point to know who we can trust."

"That one's easy. For you, there's Kathleen, and then there's me. Everyone else is a suspect."

"Even Timothy?" she asked.

"I'm afraid even Timothy," I said. I'd been thinking about it for a while, but I hadn't said anything to Annie yet. It was time.

"You're serious, aren't you?" she asked me, clearly troubled by the thought.

"It was his land they were digging on, and you heard him as well as I did. He left class early to come home, but do we really know how *early* he left? I know you don't like thinking about it, but what if he came back even sooner than he claims, found them digging on his land, had a fight with Bones, and killed him?"

"First off, Timothy doesn't have that kind of temper," she said, defending her new boyfriend. "And secondly, he wouldn't dump Bones's body in my pond, even if he did kill him."

"What if the two events weren't related, though?" I asked her.

"Why would someone work so hard to get rid of his body if they didn't kill him in the first place?"

"What if they thought they were protecting the real murderer?" I asked.

"I don't see it, Pat. You've got to be wrong."

"Maybe I am, but we still need to look into it."

"I don't know. I need some time to think," Annie said as she headed for the door.

"Are you sure you don't want to stay?" I knew that what I'd said had troubled her, but she'd needed to hear it.

"No offense, but if it's all the same to you, I'd rather be alone."

Once Annie was gone, I began to regret some of the things I'd said, not because I didn't think they were possibilities, but because I'd clearly hurt my twin sister by saying them. I knew that once she had a chance to mull over what I'd said, she'd realize that it was important to consider all of the possibilities, no matter where those paths led us.

I just hoped she'd get over it soon.

Being at odds with her was painful for me, made even worse by the fact that there was a killer on the loose.

CHAPTER 13: ANNIE

MY BROTHER WAS BEING RIDICULOUS. At least that's what I kept telling myself as I left the Iron and headed for my cabin, despite his protests that I should stay there with him. The very idea that Timothy could have had anything to do with the murder and/or the body being dumped in my pond was too wild to even consider. Why would he do such a thing? And then something Pat had said struck home. I knew that on rare occasions, Timothy could have a bit of a temper, particularly if it was over something territorial. Could he have come back early, found Bones desecrating his land by digging it up, and then struck the man down in a fit of anger? I didn't like to even consider the possibility; it didn't fit into my picture of the man. For argument's sake, I tried to figure out of if it were possible; not probable, not likely, just feasible. Pat and I had grown to believe recently that given enough motivation, just about anyone could find themselves in a position where they felt forced to take another life. It wasn't a pretty part of the human psyche, but it was there, whether we liked it or not. But Timothy? Dear sweet Timothy whose embrace made me feel so safe when so many others had failed? A killer? No matter how I felt about the man, I had to acknowledge that my brother was right. My new boyfriend needed to be on our list of suspects, regardless of my feelings toward him. I loved my brother, forever and always, but I didn't necessarily always have to like him, and at the moment, he was far from my most favorite person in the world.

The crime scene tape around the pond's edge near my cabin didn't help matters. The garish yellow tape with bold black letters seemed to shout as it destroyed the visual tranquility of my homestead. Maybe Pat had been right about that as well. I probably should have stayed with him in the upstairs bedroom at the Iron, but I hadn't been able to bring myself to do it. Besides, I'd needed to be alone long enough to examine my thoughts and feelings. Doing my best to ignore the yellow tape and, more importantly, what it represented, I let myself into the cabin and built a fire. The evenings had a distinct chill to them now, and I knew that cold weather wasn't that far away. At the moment, I wished for a blanket of snow over everything, washing away the details of the world around me in swaths of white, hiding the ugliness around me. Then again, there wasn't enough snow in the world to disguise what someone had done to Bones. Settling in by the fire, I found myself drifting off despite the dark thoughts flying through my mind, and when I woke up the next morning, I was startled to see that I'd spent the night on my couch, even though my loft bed was just a few feet away. I'd had a restless night's sleep, and I wasn't really in any shape to face the world, but unfortunately, the world had other plans, so I got up, showered, put on fresh clothes, and headed back into the Iron.

Pat was waiting for me out on the front porch. "Annie, I wanted to talk to you about how we left things last night," he said. The man was clearly as miserable as I was, and I doubted that he'd gotten much more sleep, either.

"I'm the one who's sorry," I said, simple and straight to the point. "You were right. Timothy has to be a suspect. Personal feelings shouldn't matter."

"I wouldn't say they don't matter," Pat said. "We just can't let them rule us. I still should have been more sensitive to the way you felt than I was. The last thing I want on this earth is to ever hurt you, Annie. In case I don't tell you enough, you're not just my twin sister; you're my best friend."

I smiled at him as I mounted the few steps and hugged him. "I feel the exact same way about you, Pat."

We held our embrace for nearly a minute, and as I pulled away, I asked, "Are you hungry? I haven't had breakfast, and there's time for me to make us something before we open the shop for the day."

"I could cook for you," he said, clearly still trying to make amends.

I wasn't exactly sure that his cooking would help matters any, though. "Tell you what. Let me say that I appreciate your kind offer, but it's still my grill. I'd be just as happy doing the cooking."

"Happier, I'd guess," he said with a grin, and I knew that things were right between us again.

"Happier," I echoed. "What sounds good to you?"

"How about one of your famous scrambles?" he asked.

"I think that sounds great. I don't have time to make biscuits, though. Will toast do?"

He feigned disappointment. "I suppose it will have to."

"If you can wait until we open our doors to the public, I'll be able to make you your biscuits." It was a hollow offer, and he knew it.

"If we wait until then, I won't get to eat until eleven or twelve."

"If then," I said with a smile.

"You know what? Toast sounds great!"

"I thought it might," I said as we went inside. I headed straight for my area and scrounged around in the fridge before I even got the eggs out. I found some bacon, ham, and sausage left over from the day before. It seemed that we were destined to have a meat lover's scramble today. Whipping up five eggs, I lit one of the burners and grabbed a large omelet pan. Not waiting for the eggs to set, I then added the meats, crumbling everything in turn, and then I proceeded to scramble the eggs, along with the extras that I'd added as well. Pat had once called it an ugly omelet, and I'd been a little miffed by his description, so that day I'd had it all to myself, despite being so stuffed I could barely get another bite down. Since then, they'd been known as scrambles, and we shared this one over coffee, finishing up just before Skip and Edith arrived for the day. The apologies had taken care of the momentary rift between my brother and me, while the scramble had sealed the deal. We were back on good terms, all the way, and I found myself bracing for the day's activities. We were going to not only run the Iron together today, but we were also going to try to find out what had really happened to Bones and why. It was a tall order, but if anyone could do it, I knew that we could.

"Heads up," Pat said a little after nine as he walked by the grill. I looked around to see what he was talking about. Carter Hayes had just come in, and he was heading straight for his mail.

"I'll be right back," I told the three customers waiting for their orders.

"Annie, how long is it going to be? I've got to get to work." Thad Jennings, a construction worker who liked to have a late breakfast at the Iron just about every day, was frowning at me as he said it, tapping his wrist where a watch would be if he'd worn one.

I grabbed a piece of bacon I'd fried up earlier and slapped it between two pieces of dry toast. "There you go."

"Hey, this isn't what I ordered," Thad protested. He'd asked for a sausage omelet, which I well knew, since it was his steady breakfast request.

"I know that, but I'd hate for you to be late for work," I said with a grin. I turned to the other two customers. "Anyone else in a hurry?"

"No, ma'am."

"I'm good."

"Great," I said. I glanced back at Thad. "I thought you were late. You'd better start eating."

"You know what? They can wait for me," he said.

I smiled, taking the poor substitute for a meal back from him. "Like I said, I won't be a minute, and then I'll make you a real breakfast."

"Take your time," Thad said, avoiding all eye contact with me.

I knew that I'd been a little harsh with him, so I patted him on the back as I walked past him. "I'm glad you can stick around. I appreciate that."

"My pleasure," he said with a genuine smile. "I've been trying to get Jay to take over more responsibilities on the job site. This will be a good test for him."

"I'm happy I could help," I said, then I joined Pat. Carter was just opening his mailbox when I caught up with my brother, and he looked absolutely startled when he turned around and found us both staring at him. It was time for us to have a little chat, whether Carter knew it or not.

"Hey, Pat; hi Annie. What's up?" he asked us, clearly a little startled to find us both focusing on him. As a nervous tic, Carter pulled off his thick glasses and cleaned them with his bandana, something that I'd seen him do enough before to realize that something was on his mind.

"How's it going, Carter?" I asked him as he glanced at his mail. It looked like all junk to me.

"Fine. Well, I'll see you both around."

He started to walk away when Pat stepped in front of him, not necessarily in a menacing way, but it was clear that we wanted to speak with him, and he didn't have much choice in the matter. "We heard you had a run-in with some kids yesterday," Pat said.

"No, not that I recall," Carter said as he tried to get around my brother.

"Are you trying to say that you weren't on Timothy Roberts's land yesterday and told some kids that it belonged to you?" I asked him.

Carter frowned for a moment as he pushed his glasses back onto the bridge of his nose. It was pretty clear that we'd caught him in a lie, and I was curious to see how he was going to try to worm his way out of it. "Oh, that."

"Yes, that," I said.

"I wanted to talk to Timothy about something," Carter said. "We were supposed to meet out on his land, but I found these kids digging up the ground when I got there instead. That's why I ran them off. I didn't figure they'd listen to me if I didn't claim that the property belonged to me, but I didn't mean anything by it."

"There's just one problem with that, Carter," Pat said.

"What's that?"

"Timothy was out of town when you had that confrontation with those college kids," I told him, studying him carefully for a reaction to being caught. "There's no way that he would have scheduled a meeting with you at that time."

"I don't know where you're getting your information, Annie, but that's not the case at all. I saw him yesterday just after lunch, and we made plans to get together out on his land. I wanted to hire on as a helper when he cut down enough trees to carve out his new homestead. He stood me up, though."

"Funny, but Timothy hasn't mentioned any of that to me," I said.

Carter looked a little sly as he asked me, "Do you honestly think your new boyfriend is going to run everything he does past you first before he does it? I'd be amazed if there was a *lot* you didn't know, Annie."

"Don't try to change the subject," Pat said. I was shaken by Carter's statement. Could Timothy really be keeping things from me? My life was an open book, and I'd just naturally assumed that his was as well. Had I been wrong about that from the start?

Pat continued, "Carter, you know the first thing we're going to do is check with Timothy to see if that's true or not."

"Suit yourself," Carter said as he sidestepped Pat and headed for the door. "You'll see that I'm not lying to you about that or anything else."

As soon as Carter left, I grabbed my phone.

Timothy didn't answer, though. He could have been with a client with his accounting firm.

Then again, he could just be ignoring me.

At the prompt for a message, I said, "This is Annie. Call me the second you get this."

"That was kind of cold, wasn't it?" Pat asked me after I finished my message.

"Pat, he told me that he didn't come back until later yesterday. You know that I can't stand being lied to."

"Annie, this might all just be a simple misunderstanding. Timothy might have slipped when he told you, or you might have remembered it wrong." I looked at him steadily for a few moments before my twin brother added, "Okay, you're not likely to be the one who made a mistake, but it doesn't mean that Timothy's been lying to you."

"I suppose we'll find that out when he calls back," I said.

Ten minutes later, the man himself came into the Iron with a troubled look on his face.

"What was that message all about?" he asked me.

"You didn't have to rush over here," I said calmly, and then I glanced over at Pat. He knew that my tranquil demeanor was a storm warning sign if ever there was one. Timothy had better start treading lightly if he knew what was good for him.

"You sounded so cold that I was afraid not to," Timothy said. "Whatever I've done, I apologize and beg you for your forgiveness."

He'd tried to make light of the serious tenor of my mood, but I wasn't having it. "When exactly did you get back into town yesterday?"

"I already told you that," Timothy said, looking instantly uncomfortable.

"As a matter of fact, you were a little vague about the exact time you got back," I reminded him. Pat knew when to be quiet, so I knew that he wasn't going to say a word until this was resolved, one way or the other.

"What does it matter what the exact time was?" Timothy asked, clearly a little unhappy about my line of questioning.

"It matters to me. Isn't that enough for you?"

He frowned and then nodded. "Okay, so maybe I'd been back a little longer than I might have let on. I was eager to get the ball rolling on clearing my homestead."

"So you went to your property while the kids were still there, before we all went together?" I asked him icily. If it were true, it was a lie of a much greater magnitude than simply glossing over a particular time. He'd appeared to be honestly surprised by finding those holes on his land. Had he been lying about that as well?

"No!" Timothy must have realized that he'd spoken a little louder than was called for. We got the attention of everyone in the Iron, including my patiently waiting diners at the grill. In a lower voice, he added, "I was supposed to meet Carter Hayes in town. He wants to help me clear part of my land, but he never showed up. I gave up on him when he stood me up, grabbed a quick sandwich at home, and then I went straight out to my land and found you two there."

"Carter claims that was where you were supposed to meet him in the first place," Pat said.

"You've spoken with him about me?" Timothy asked, clearly unhappy about it.

"Don't blame my brother. We both did, Timothy," I said.

My boyfriend looked at me carefully before he spoke. "Annie, am I a suspect here?"

"You'd have to ask Kathleen about that," I said, trying to avoid answering his direct question.

"Trust me, I will, but right now, I'm asking you. Do you think it's possible that I killed that kid, just for digging a few holes on my property?"

Pat tried to save me from answering by speaking up. "Timothy, everyone who might have been out there needs to be cleared. You own that land. It just makes sense to get your alibi so we can eliminate you."

Pat had tried to help, but ultimately, he'd only made it worse. Timothy bridled at the word "alibi." "I've already told you the truth," he said to my brother icily, and then he looked back at me. "Well? Do you think I'm capable of committing murder, Annie?"

"Just about everyone is, given the right circumstances," Pat tried to add.

Timothy wasn't having any of it. "Patrick, if you don't mind, I'd like to hear what your sister has to say."

"Given the right circumstances, yes, I do." My voice was nearly a whisper as I spoke, but I couldn't bring myself to lie to him, no matter what it might end up costing me.

"I'm sorry. What did you just say?" Timothy asked me, though I knew that he'd heard me the first time.

"I said that it's possible. You *have* to be a suspect, but then in Kathleen's eyes, I'm sure that I'm one as well."

"Frankly, I don't care what your sister thinks, even if she is the sheriff. I understand why she might want to know where I was at the time of the murder, but I didn't think that you'd have to." Timothy turned and walked away, not in any particular hurry, but not lingering, either.

"Say something to him, Annie," Pat said urgently.

"What is there to say? I couldn't lie to him."

"At least stop him before he leaves. You can't let him go believing that you don't trust him."

"Pat, I don't have any choice. He got back earlier than he implied yesterday, it was his land being trespassed on, and we both know how protective Timothy can be about the things he cares about."

"Including you," Pat reminded me.

"Maybe before, but it appears that's changed now."

"Don't give up that easily," Pat said. "He's perfect for you, and you can't let our murder investigation get in the way of your life."

"Then let's solve this as quickly as we can," I said. "But know this. I'm not dropping this case, and neither are you. We've known from the very beginning that we were going to burn some bridges if we started digging into other people's lives."

"I realize that, but I never thought for one second that one of your bridges was going to explode in your face," Pat said.

"Trust me, I'm not happy about it either, but until I can look Timothy in the eye and tell him that I know he didn't do it, there's nothing I can do about it."

"Then let's keep digging, and do it fast," Pat said.

CHAPTER 14: PAT

WE DIDN'T HAVE TIME TO do any more investigating at the moment, though. As much as I loved running the Iron with Annie, it had a tendency of getting in the way of our unofficial inquiries from time to time. There was a steady stream of customers throughout the rest of the day—both up front where I was in charge and back at Annie's grill—and we didn't have much of a chance to even compare notes between the two of us. The college student's death had understandably made waves in Maple Crest, but not as much as it would have if he'd been local. It wasn't because anyone cared less that someone had lost their life; it was due more to the fact that no one had known Bones. That made his homicide a little more faceless than if it had been someone who'd lived among us. This was almost like a murder far away in Charlotte or Raleigh, disassociated from our daily lives. The fact that it had occurred on Timothy's land, and right next to Annie's, made it newsworthy, but without any real fuel to feed the flames of speculation, it just wasn't the same. I was still wondering what our approach should be when I was surprised to see all four surviving members of the treasure-hunting expedition show up at the Iron a little before noon.

"Hi, Peggy," I said as I approached her first. "How are you feeling today?"

"I'm upset about Bones, but at least I know that I'm not losing my mind, so that's something, anyway," she said. "When he vanished like that, I was beginning to have my doubts."

"How long have you been discharged from the hospital?" I asked her.

"It just happened. The doctor wouldn't release me until I had another interview with your sister. I couldn't tell her anything new, so she finally agreed to let me go. The first thing I wanted to do was get some of your sister's excellent cooking after suffering through the food there, so we all headed straight over here."

"How did you get here?" I asked Henry. "Did you all come in the car?"

"The sheriff released the van back to us around ten this morning," he told me. "Man, she's tough, isn't she?"

"Why do you say that?"

"No disrespect intended, but I *knew* that I was innocent and she still managed to scare me."

"I wouldn't take it personally if I were you. She considers it a personal affront that someone committed murder in her jurisdiction," I said. "What are you all going to do now?"

"I guess we're hanging around Maple Crest a little longer, since we can't leave town just yet," Marty said, "not that I was shocked when the sheriff told us."

"Don't misunderstand us. We want to cooperate," Gretchen added. "After all, Bones was with us. Julian, I should say."

"Did Kathleen find out his real name?" I asked her.

"The news came in this morning. He'd been fingerprinted for something somewhere along the line, and it popped up in her database. His real name was Julian Valentine Bonetti."

That explained why the student had gone by Bones. It had less to do with his pre-med line of studies than it did a trifecta of unusual names. "Did she happen to mention if they'd notified his next of kin yet?"

"From what we heard, all that's left is his father, and he's on some kind of expedition right now where he can't be contacted. They're expecting him back next week, so until then, we're all supposed to keep it under our hats."

"I'm kind of surprised your sister didn't tell you this already," Marty said snidely.

"You'd be amazed by what she decides not to share with Annie and me," I answered.

"Pat, I'd love to chat, but I'm so hungry right now that I could eat the bark off of a tree," Peggy said. "Do you mind if we have lunch?"

"No, of course not," I said. I had more questions to ask them, but at least my twin sister was going to get a crack at them herself. I knew that Annie wouldn't let an opportunity to interview so many of our suspects at one time pass her by. I just hoped she'd be able to get more out of them than I'd been able to.

Peggy walked back to the grill, with Gretchen and Marty close on her heels. Henry stayed back, and once the group was out of earshot, he said, "I'd appreciate it if you'd take it easy on Peggy, Pat. I understand that you want to find out what happened, but you need to remember that she's been through a lot over the past twenty-four hours."

"I get that," I said. "How did you happen to find out that she was being discharged?"

Henry smiled. "Actually, your sister told us when she handed me the keys to the van. She's not really a bad sort, is she?"

"Not if you didn't do anything," I said. "If you're innocent, you won't find a better advocate to deal with in law enforcement."

"Yeah, I totally get that," Henry replied. "Well, I'd better get back to the group."

"When you're finished with your lunch, would you mind if we chatted a little more?" I asked him.

"I'm not sure what I could tell you that I haven't already said," Henry replied. "You still think one of us did it, don't you?"

"I don't know yet," I answered him honestly. "That's one of the reasons that I'd like to continue our conversation."

Henry took a step back. "With me? Do you think I killed Bones?"

"I didn't say that."

"But you believe it's a possibility, don't you?" Henry was clearly troubled by the prospect of being one of our suspects.

"If it makes you feel any better, you four aren't the only people we're looking at," I said.

"So you *are* investigating the murder," Henry said with a frown. "Does your sister know what you're doing?"

"You'd better believe it. I tell Annie everything," I said.

"I'm not talking about that sister," he said.

"Yes, Kathleen is well aware of the fact that we're doing a little investigating on our own."

"If you don't mind me asking, why are you so interested in what happened to Bones?" Henry asked, clearly genuinely curious about our motivation. "He was a stranger to you until we came to town."

"Maybe so, but it happened on land that belongs to a friend of ours, not to mention the fact that it also abuts Annie's, and then someone had the audacity to dump the body in her pond. Are you honestly all that surprised that we'd take an active interest in what happened to Bones, I mean Julian?"

"If you call him that, nobody will know what you're talking about," Henry said with the hint of a grin, despite the serious nature of our conversation.

"Bones it is," I said.

"Who else are you looking at as suspects?" Henry asked me.

"I'm not sure that I'm ready to share that information with the general public yet," I said, hedging my bets.

"We're not exactly casual observers here, Pat. We have a stake in this as well."

"I understand that, but I still think it would be better if we kept our list to ourselves, at least for the time being."

"Okay, I can respect that, but listen, if there's anything that we can do to help you find the killer, all you have to do is ask. The four of us have a bigger stake in this than you do."

"Even if helping us means that you end up implicating someone in your group?" I asked him.

Henry frowned at the thought as he stared at his companions, who were all watching us at the moment.

"I don't think that's going to happen."

"But if it does?" I pressed him a little harder.

"When all is said and done, I want to know what really happened to Bones. No matter what."

"And if Peggy or Gretchen did it, you'll help us catch them?"

"Hey, it could have just as easily been Marty," Henry said.

"Why do you believe that?"

"I'm just saying, we all had the opportunity to sneak back to where Bones was and clobber him, but that means that someone else did, too. We were pretty spread out that day looking for the outside parameters of our digging zone. Anyone could have whacked Bones with that pickaxe, including a perfect stranger to us."

"I understand that, but then motivation becomes the question, doesn't it?" I asked him. "Who else had a reason?"

Henry shook his head. "That's all that I've been able to think about since Peggy found Bones's body. What if he found the hoarded money while the rest of us were off other places? Someone could have spotted him getting it, confronted him about it, and then killed him for it."

"That sounds like an awfully big coincidence to me, that someone just happened along at exactly the right time."

"Not if they'd been watching us from the woods all along," Henry said softly.

"Do you have any reason to suspect that was the case?" I asked him.

"We saw some signs that someone might have been out there. You know, a tree branch snapping, a light we couldn't explain at night, that kind of thing. I had the creepiest feeling that someone was keeping tabs on us, waiting and hoping that we'd find something. If that's the case, we'll never find the real killer."

"There's another possibility that you haven't considered in that scenario," I reminded him.

"What am I missing?"

"One of your crew could have been secretly watching just as easily. If Bones made a discovery, would he necessarily tell any of you about it?"

Henry pondered that for a few moments, and then he shook his head. "Maybe not. Since his dad was financing the trip, he might have felt entitled to keep the money all for himself."

"What would happen if one of you caught him taking it?"

"There would be trouble, there's no doubt about that," Henry said.

"So, the question remains, who might have done it?"

"I still don't think any of us murdered him," he said.

"I can understand you feeling that way," I replied, "but until we learn something that eliminates one or all of you as suspects, we have to keep digging."

"I get that," Henry said, and then he stuck out his hand. "Are we still good?"

"We are," I said, shaking it.

"Excellent. Then if you'll excuse me, I'm going to go eat."

"I'd recommend it," I said with a grin. I didn't think that Henry was the killer, though I'd been surprised before. Still, I liked him, and I hoped fervently that he wasn't playing me for a fool.

CHAPTER 15: ANNIE

"What would you like to eat?" I asked Peggy as she studied the menu. "I've eaten hospital food before myself, so I know that you must be famished."

"You have no idea," she said with a grin. "What's good today?"

"Would you be surprised if I told you that everything I serve is delightful?" I asked with a grin of my own, which was my usual response to the query. "But if you've got the appetite for it, the beef ribs are particularly good today. They include a side of baby carrots, new potatoes, peas, onions, and green peppers, all simmered for hours in one of my cast iron Dutch ovens."

"I'll take two helpings," she said as she shoved the menu aside.

"Don't get me wrong, I'll be more than happy to serve you anything you'd like, but if you might take the suggestion, start out with one order. If you're still hungry, the second will be hot."

"Sure. That sounds good. Do you have any bread to go along with it?"

"I've got spicy cornbread and a cheddar chive bread that I'm particularly proud of, both made right here in my kitchen."

"I can't decide, they both sound so good," she said.

"How about a slice of each?" I offered.

"Sold."

I nodded, and then turned to the others. "How about you three?"

"That all sounds wonderful to me," Henry said.

Gretchen nodded. "Make it three."

I turned to Marty. "Care to make it four?"

He frowned as he shook his head. "No, thanks. I'll have a burger."

"I can do that," I said. I should have known from his demeanor alone that Marty wasn't the get along/go along kind of guy. It didn't bother me in the least that he'd have to wait for his meal. I served the others immediately, and I caught Marty staring at Gretchen's plate. "It's not too late to change your order, you know."

"No, I'm good," he said.

"Suit yourself," I said as I grabbed a hamburger patty and threw it onto the griddle. While it was cooking, I asked him, "What would you like on it?"

"Drown it in catsup and it will be fine with me," he said.

"You can handle that yourself," I said as I put a full bottle in front of him. It pained me enough to have my food desecrated in that manner, but I refused to do it myself. If he wanted it that way, that was his prerogative, but at least my hands would be clean. I used only the finest quality of everything I served at the grill. It might as well have been a tough old bull for all of the taste he was going to get out of it, but sadly, I didn't have any tough old bull on hand at the moment to use as a substitute.

As Henry, Peggy, and Gretchen ate, I studied Marty for a moment. "If you don't mind me saying so, you don't look all that happy about being here."

"Do you say that to all of your customers?" he snapped at me.

"Just the ones who look miserable," I answered with a smile.

"The truth of the matter is that I want to leave this dump the second your sister lets me," he said.

"I can't address your problems with Maple Crest, but if you don't want to eat in here, I can make it to go and you can eat out in the parking lot."

Gretchen frowned at Marty before she spoke. "I've told you before that you need to behave yourself, Marty."

"Sorry," he mumbled.

It was amazing to get any apology out of him at all. He really must have had a thing for Gretchen to stoop so low as to tell me he was sorry about anything.

"He didn't want to come in the first place," Gretchen explained to me.

"Really? Then why did you?" I asked Marty, though I was fairly certain of the answer. It was pretty clear from where I was standing that Gretchen herself was the main reason he'd come, despite the possibility of buried treasure.

"I didn't think there'd be much use for my specialty, given the state of that map," he said, "and I was right. If we'd been looking for a shipwreck, I might have been needed, but using a cartographer for the map Blankenship left was like using a cannon to kill a fly."

"You helped determine the exact site, though. That was important," Gretchen said, obviously trying to buoy his spirits. Was there a little interest on her part as well?

"Any one of you could have done that just by walking the property," he said. "The well's there, and so is the foundation of the original house, not to mention the family cemetery. The place might as well have had searchlights marking it."

"Don't be so hard on yourself," Gretchen said.

I turned to flip his burger and toast the bun I was about to serve it on, and when I looked back, Gretchen was patting his shoulder. I glanced over at Henry and Peggy to see what they thought of this development, but they might as well have been someplace else. They seemed to only care about each other, and I had a hunch that if Peggy had killed Bones, Henry would have helped her hide the body without a single bit of hesitation. Pat and I hadn't considered the possibility that two of them could have been working together, but it was something that I needed to mention to my brother later.

"Did any of you see anything out of place yesterday at the site?" I asked them.

"What do you mean?" Henry asked.

"Was there anything odd or unusual? In particular, was there something there that shouldn't have been there, or maybe there was something that *should* have been there that was gone? Anything might help, no matter how big or small."

"Somebody was watching us from the woods," Gretchen said softly.

"What? Why didn't you say anything to me about it?" Marty wanted to know.

"I saw him, too," Henry said. "At least I think it was a guy."

"I didn't see anyone," Marty said. "Did you?" he asked Peggy.

"No, not at the site. I did nearly hit a gray pickup truck when I pulled out onto the road to get help, though."

I wanted to know about this mysterious watcher, but I had to address Peggy's observation first. "Did you say gray?"

"Yes, there's no doubt in my mind. He was so close to me that I nearly hit him, and I had the feeling that he'd been parked off to the side of the road just waiting for me to come out."

Timothy drove a gray truck, but then so did a great many other folks in the area. Well, not a great many exactly, but I did know of at least four other trucks that matched that general description. "Was there anything else unusual about it?" I asked her. "Think hard. It could be important."

"The rear bumper had a bunch of stickers on it," she said. "Sorry. I didn't get a good look at who was driving it. It could have been Elvis for all I know."

"Do you remember any of the stickers?" Her description still didn't eliminate every other gray truck in town, but it was getting closer.

"Sorry. All I caught was something about lumber."

I felt my skin grow icy. "Could it have been 'Lumberjacks Do It In The Woods'?"

"I don't know. It might have. Like I said, I only saw it for a split second."

I had a feeling that it had indeed been Timothy. If it had been, though, why had he been waiting for her to leave the site? To collect the body and move it, perhaps? Or was there some other, simpler explanation? If there was, I didn't have a clue what it might be. Whether

I liked it or not, it was something else that I'd have to discuss with Pat.

"Let's get back to whoever was watching you from the woods," I said. "Were you able to get any impressions about who it might possibly be?"

"I didn't get a good look at whoever it was, and besides, I don't really know anybody around here," Gretchen said.

"I'm not asking you to make a positive identification," I said. "Just tell me anything that stands out in your mind."

"Well, I know for a fact that he wore glasses," Gretchen said. "I'm pretty sure that I saw some reflections off his lenses."

"I didn't see that," Henry said.

"That doesn't mean that it's not true," Gretchen said defensively.

"Of course it doesn't," Henry added.

"Henry, you say that you didn't notice whether he was wearing glasses or not, but did you see anything specific?" I asked him.

"No, at first I thought my eyes were playing tricks on me. By the time I decided that I was seeing something more than shadows, whoever was there was gone. I looked around and saw a little trampled grass later, but that's about it."

"And you didn't see fit to tell the rest of us about it?" Marty asked as I slid his finished burger in front of him. Much to my dismay, he emptied half the catsup bottle on it, and I couldn't even bring myself to watch him take a bite.

"I said something to Bones," Henry said. "He decided that there was no use panicking everyone else with it, so I kept my mouth shut."

"I guess that makes you an accessory, doesn't it?" Marty asked hotly.

"Marty!" Gretchen scolded him openly. "That's uncalled for."

"It's true, though, isn't it?" Marty asked defiantly. "If Henry had told the rest of us about what he'd seen, maybe we could have been more vigilant, and none of this would have ever happened."

"Based on your logic, that makes me an accessory, too, then," Gretchen said softly.

"I didn't mean it that way," he said.

"It's still true, though. If Henry failed because he kept what he'd seen to himself, then so did I. At least he told Bones. I didn't even do that."

"It's not your fault," Henry said as he patted Gretchen's shoulder, something that both Peggy and Marty weren't happy with.

"Thanks for saying that," Gretchen told him.

Henry smiled at her, and then Peggy spoke up. "The fact of the matter is that none of us were responsible for what happened to Bones. The only person who bears any blame is the one who murdered him with that pickaxe."

I didn't want to point out that those folks weren't exactly mutually exclusive, but I decided that there was enough conflict going on at the moment as it was. Maybe there was a way we could play them off each other, but I wasn't about to pursue that until we'd eliminated all of our other suspects. A thought occurred to me after considering Gretchen's observation that the watcher had been wearing glasses. So far, the only person involved who wore spectacles on a regular basis that I knew of was Carter Hayes. He'd been awfully glib about throwing Timothy under the bus when we'd questioned him earlier.

I wondered how he'd react if we told him that we suspected that he'd been keeping tabs on the treasure hunters since they'd first arrived.

CHAPTER 16: PAT

UNFORTUNATELY, THE FOUR COLLEGE KIDS ate and left the Iron before I had a chance to speak with any of them again. Hopefully Annie had been able to find something else out, but I wouldn't be able to catch up with her until we had a lull. Unfortunately, for the rest of the day, there were no lulls.

"Hey, Pat, I can work some overtime if you need me to hang around and help out," Skip told me a few minutes before we were set to close.

"Thanks, but I think we have everything under control."

"I really don't mind," he insisted.

This was clearly about more than just helping us out at the store. "What's going on, Skip?"

"Nothing."

From his dour expression, I could tell that wasn't entirely true. "Come on. Are you short on cash at the moment?"

Skip looked uncomfortable, but finally, he admitted, "Kind of. I'm saving up to buy a welding rig, but I'm not having much luck."

"I didn't know you could weld."

"I can't," he said with a grin, "but when has the lack of knowledge ever stopped me from doing something in the past?"

"Do you honestly believe that it's something you can just pick up?" I asked him. "I think that might be a dangerous way to learn."

"I can read a book first, and if I have any questions, I can always ask Kilmer Jacks. He's a crackerjack welder."

Kilmer came into the Iron most days, more often for Annie's food than what I had to offer up front. He was a large man, with wild brown hair and a full beard. "Have you asked him about your plans?"

"Why would I do that? I don't even have any welding stuff yet."

"I mean to teach you before you get your own equipment. He still teaches adult education classes at the community college, doesn't he?"

"I have no idea, but I can't see myself doing that. That's just for old people. No disrespect intended," he added hastily.

Did he really think of me as being all that much older than he was? I might have had twelve years on him, but I hadn't realized that made me ancient in his eyes. "Why don't you take the class first to see if you enjoy doing it? If you can't afford that, I'll be glad to pay your tuition myself."

"I couldn't let you do that," he said. "Besides, those classes probably are pretty cheap."

I grinned at him. "Why do you think I offered to pay? Seriously, if you take the class, maybe you can weld something for me at the Iron someday."

"Like what?" he asked, returning my smile.

"I don't know, but I'm sure that I'll think of something. Go on and make the call."

"Okay. Thanks." A minute later, he came back, grinning broadly. "You were right. He's teaching a class, and it starts this week. It's just thirty bucks, plus supplies, so I can cover that myself."

"I really don't mind," I said.

"I know, but this way, if I ever do have to weld something for you, I can charge you full price for the job," he said, smiling.

I had to laugh. The young man had an entrepreneurial spirit that just wouldn't die. "Fair enough. Did you finish restocking the canned goods section?"

"No, but I'm on it right now, so consider it done," he said.

Skip finished up in record time, and soon enough, the doors were both locked and the Iron was closed for the day. I'd done most of my work earlier, since we hadn't had any customers toward the end, so I had the deposit ready when I walked back to the grill, where I found Annie scrubbing the iron griddle with a stone of some sort. "Need a hand with anything back here?" I asked her.

"No, I'm good. How did you manage to finish up so early?"

"It was easy. I cheated," I replied with a smile.

"I would have done that myself, but people kept coming in and demanding that I feed them," she answered.

"Don't you just hate when that happens?"

"What was your conversation with Skip about?" she asked me. "He seemed pretty animated, so I bet it wasn't about work."

"He wants to learn how to weld," I said.

Annie laughed. "That boy is going to be dangerous someday with the amount of knowledge he acquires on a monthly basis."

"I'd rather think of him as being well rounded. It helps me sleep better at night," I said. "Did you happen to get anything out of our group of suspects while they were back here having a meal?"

"Yes, and I've been dying to catch you up to speed on what I found out. Gretchen and Henry both spotted someone watching them from the woods. She saw someone wearing glasses, but Henry didn't. Who do we know who's attached to this investigation and wears glasses?"

"Carter Hayes," I said. "That's kind of creepy, isn't it? Do you think he was there watching the girls?"

"No, and eww, by the way. Thanks for putting that thought into my head. I think he was more interested in what they were looking for."

"How could he possibly know what they were up to?" I asked her.

"I don't know. He could have seen something, or maybe he overheard them talking. If he was lingering on my land, you'd better believe that I'm going to find out what he was up to."

"We can track him down as soon as we make our bank deposit, if you're free this evening," I said. It was my subtle way of asking her if she was going to try to find Timothy so she could patch things up with him, but I wasn't about to just come right out and ask her.

"I don't have any plans whatsoever," Annie said.

"Are you sure?"

She knew what I'd been getting at. "Patrick, I'm the last person on earth he wants to talk to right now."

"Maybe that's the best reason of all to find him and clear things up," I urged her gently. "The longer you wait, the harder it's going to be."

"What can I say to him right now, though? I still believe that he's a viable suspect, no matter how unlikely it might be, so I can't mend what's broken until I can face him and tell him that I no longer think he's potentially a killer. Until then, I'm going to avoid him as much as I can."

"Does that really sound like solid logic to you, Annie?"

"It doesn't matter how it sounds. It's what I'm doing."

I could tell that I wasn't getting anything else out of my twin sister. "Did you learn anything else from the group?"

"I'm not sure. Maybe. The more I think about it, the more I feel as though it's probably not important," Annie said after some hesitation.

"Why don't you tell me, and then I can decide for myself," I said.

"Fine. Peggy claimed that she nearly hit a truck as she left the dig site after finding Bones's body. She claimed that she had to slam on her brakes to keep from hitting the other vehicle."

"Did she happen to see who was driving?"

"No, but she did a good job describing the truck. It was gray, and it had the word 'lumber' on a bumper sticker."

"As in 'Lumberjacks Do It In The Woods'?"

"Maybe, but she wasn't sure," Annie said.

I couldn't just let it go, no matter how much my sister might want me to. "That means that Timothy was out at his land much earlier than we thought before."

"Not necessarily. There's one more thing," Annie said.

"What's that?"

"I've been giving it some serious thought, and I believe that there's a slight possibility that two or more of them could have been working together," she said softly.

"Why do you think that?"

"Henry is clearly close to Peggy. If he thought she killed Bones, he might get rid of the body in order to protect her. It's also pretty clear that Marty is infatuated with Gretchen, though I don't know if she feels that way about him. She seems to be playing both men off each other, something that Peggy spotted easily enough. The same logic works for Gretchen and Marty as it does for Henry and Peggy."

"The women could be covering for the men too, you know," I pointed out.

"I know that," Annie said.

"That means we have six suspects at the moment, and a variety of combinations," I said. As I ticked off fingers, I added the names aloud, "Henry, Marty, Gretchen, Peggy, Carter, and Timothy. I'm sorry about adding his name, but like you just said yourself, it has to be there until we can eliminate him from our list."

"I don't know about you, but I still don't have a clue as to which one of them might have done it," Annie said, "Though some of them are less likely than the rest. I can't see Timothy killing anyone, and Henry doesn't seem the type, either. Marty is too easy as a choice, and so is Carter. Could Gretchen or Peggy have done it? It's possible, but I have a hard time believing a woman could use a pickaxe like that."

"I wish I shared your doubts, but if one of them were threatened, defending themselves is a possibility we have to take into account, and that's even if we eliminate greed as a factor."

"Do you think Bones actually found the money?" Annie asked me.

"I don't know, but we have to assume that it's possible. Greed is an awfully powerful motive. Someone, especially if they were broke, might not be able to quell their impulse to steal the money, even if it meant assaulting, and ultimately killing, the young man who uncovered it."

"It might explain Carter's behavior," she said. "You know how tightfisted he is. If he saw that kind of silver and gold, he might do anything it took to get it for himself."

"But Timothy has a good job and makes a nice living," I reminded her. "He doesn't need the money, certainly not enough to kill someone for it."

"There could be more than greed working as his motive," Annie said. "Bones could have set him off if Timothy found him digging up his land. Can you imagine them not having a confrontation if Timothy somehow discovered what was going on? I don't like to think about someone I'm dating that way, but I can't seem to get it out of my mind."

"Before we talk to Carter, should we tell Kathleen everything that you found out?" I asked my twin.

"Why don't we wait a bit first," she suggested.

"How is Kathleen going to react when she discovers that we acted on information we received before we shared it with her?"

"Fine. I'll call her," Annie said a bit testily.

"Maybe you've got a point. I don't suppose it would hurt if we waited until *after* we've spoken with Carter," I offered.

"No, you were right the first time. We agreed to play this one by the book. Let me call her before we do anything else." Annie pulled out her phone, dialed Kathleen's number, and after a full minute, she put it away, smiling.

"She didn't pick up," Annie said happily.

"Why didn't you leave a voicemail for her?"

"You know what? That never even occurred to me. I'd call her back and do it right now, but I want to leave my line open, in case there's an emergency or something."

"I give up. You win," I said with a grin.

"You're a smart fellow, aren't you?" she asked as she patted my cheek. "Now, let's go make that deposit and then track down Carter Hayes."

"Should I drive, or should we take your truck?"

"Let me drive," she said.

"That's fine by me." I liked riding around in my sister's pickup, mostly because I enjoyed the looks she usually got driving it. Most folks expected to see some burly, bearded man behind the wheel, so when they spotted Annie wheeling it expertly around town, it never failed to make me smile. For her and, in particular, the lifestyle she'd chosen for herself, it made perfect sense. After all, living in a cabin out in the middle of the woods required the use of a truck more often than it ever would a car. Besides, she was able to easily handle that treacherous driveway of hers in her truck, something I usually hesitated tackling with my car. Not only our homes but even our modes of transportation helped define us, and I was just fine with living over the Iron instead of being out in the middle of nowhere where Annie preferred.

CHAPTER 17: ANNIE

"Hello, Timothy," I said as my boyfriend walked up to where I had parked in the bank lot. Pat was inside making his deposit, and it was just my luck that Timothy was there as well.

"Hello," he said calmly as he walked straight past me to the bank's front door without a hint of hesitation.

I couldn't take the silent treatment. I called out, "Do you have a second?"

"Is there anything really left to be said?" he asked as he turned to look at me. I could tell that he was hurt, and it killed me that there was nothing I could do about it.

"I think so. Try to look at it from our position. You came back into town before you admitted earlier, and now we find out that Peggy claims that you nearly ran her over in your truck right after she found Bones's body. Even you have to admit that it looks fishy."

"If I were a stranger, sure, but you know me, Annie. I'm not a killer."

"I'm not saying that you are," I insisted.

"Maybe not, but you aren't saying that I'm innocent, either."

"Why were you at the road near your land, and why were you doing your best to get away from the place? These questions shouldn't be hard to answer, Timothy."

"Is that it, then? Have you decided that we aren't going to work out after all, and you've completely given up on us?" The hurt was very real in his voice now.

"No! Of course not! I want to keep seeing you, Timothy."

"Well, you've got a funny way of showing it," he said as he started toward the bank's front door again. However, before he went inside, he hesitated at the entry and turned back to me. "Not that it matters, but I didn't see Peggy driving anywhere yesterday afternoon, and if I nearly ran her down as she claims, wouldn't I remember it?"

"So, you're saying that you weren't there?"

He didn't answer. Instead, he walked inside, nearly running Pat over as he entered the building.

"What was that all about?" my brother asked me. "Or do I really want to know?"

"Timothy claims that he didn't come close to running into Peggy in his truck," I said.

"Did he at least admit to being on the road around his place around then?"

"At that point, he was finished speaking with me altogether. Maybe for good."

Pat touched my shoulder lightly. "You didn't do anything wrong, Annie."

"Then why do I feel as though I did? Pat, I practically accused him of lying to me."

"You had a right to ask him about his whereabouts," Pat said.

"Did I? It's not like we have any official capacity. I didn't have to press him so hard for his alibi."

"That's what we do, isn't it?" my brother asked me.

"Maybe this time, we shouldn't have."

"Do you honestly believe that?" Pat asked as he stared into my eyes.

"No. Of course not. I just wish he wouldn't be so defensive about it."

"There I might have to agree with him," Pat replied. "I'm not sure how I'd feel if Jenna asked me for an alibi at the time of a murder, particularly if it occurred on my land."

"Are you actually taking his side over mine? Seriously?"

"Of course not," he said quickly. "I'm just saying that it's a delicate situation." Pat turned back toward the bank.

"Where are you going?"

"I'm going to have a little chat with him," Pat said. "This has got to stop."

I grabbed his arm. "Not a chance."

"Annie, you have to at least let me try. I might be able to make this better."

"You could also kill it forever," I said. "Thanks for the offer, but I'll handle it."

"Are you sure?"

"I'm positive," I answered. The last thing I needed at the moment was for my brother to act as an intermediary for me with my once, and hopefully still, boyfriend. "Let's go."

"Okay," he agreed. My twin brother was clearly happy that I'd stopped him from going inside. It was pretty clear that he hadn't been looking forward to having that particular conversation himself. "Where should we start looking for Carter Hayes?"

"Let's try his place first," I said.

"Do you know where he lives?"

"He's living over Beatrice Masterson's garage," I replied.

"How did you happen to know that?"

"I've heard her talking about how he's always late paying his rent whenever she eats at the grill."

"Then to Beatrice's we go," Pat said.

Beatrice Masterson was a member of good standing in the Ladies' Floral Society. The group of women, most of them of a certain age, was interested in much more than horticulture, though that was the primary function of their organization, at least according to their charter. Though they did all possess rather green thumbs, the women were also there to step in during times of need or duress, whether it be from a death in the family, a newborn baby, or just about anything in between. Beatrice's landscaping was immaculate, with fall flowers planted in neatly mulched beds and the green lawn cut to within a sixteenth of an inch of its recommended height. There was a detached garage and steps leading up to it from the side, where Carter Hayes now resided. As we walked up to speak with him, I wondered how Beatrice had ever come to allow the man to live there in the first place. I knew that she was a widow on a fixed income, but I was still surprised that she'd chosen Carter to be her boarder.

I knocked on the door, but there was no reply.

"Try again," Pat said.

I did as he suggested.

Still no reply.

Pat leaned forward and tried the doorknob.

To his surprise, as well as my own, it was unlocked.

"Carter, we're coming in," I said as Pat pushed the door open.

What my brother and I found inside managed to surprise us both.

"He's gone," Pat said as we both looked around the small room. There was no sign that Carter Hayes had ever even lived there. It took us all of three minutes to determine that after checking the small room that held a bed, a chair, and a desk, as well as a kitchenette and a bathroom that all fit into the same size space as a one-car garage. "You're sure he lives here, right?"

"As of yesterday he did, but it's pretty clear that he's gone now," I said as I grabbed my phone. "We need to tell Kathleen about this."

"Hang on a second," Pat said as he put a hand on my arm. "We haven't even told Kathleen that Carter is on our list of suspects. Why is she going to care that he's gone all of a sudden?"

"That's why we have to bring her up to speed now," I said. "We have to tell her everything, Pat."

"I know you're right, but that doesn't mean that I have to like it. Go on and call her, if you're willing to take the hit. You know she's not going to be happy about it, right?"

"I still have to take the chance," I said.

Our older sister answered her phone after seven rings, and when she did, she sounded a little miffed. "What is it, Annie?"

"Carter Hayes is missing," I said.

"Why should I care about that? I've got more important things on my plate right now."

"Kathleen, Carter is in this up to his eyeballs. He threw the kids off Timothy's land, claiming that it was his. Also, one of the girls claims that she saw Carter spying on them while they were digging. Finally, Timothy was talking about hiring Carter to help him clear some of his land, so it's possible Carter knows more than he's let on so far. After hearing all of that, doesn't it strike you as odd that he's missing?"

"Yes, it does," she said glumly. "How do you know for a fact that he's missing?"

"We're at his place right now above Beatrice Masterson's garage. It's been cleaned out, top to bottom."

"You shouldn't be there, Annie," Kathleen said severely.

"Why not? We came by to ask him some questions and found his door open," I said, embellishing the truth a little. It had been unlocked, at any rate. "If it weren't for us, you wouldn't even know that his sudden disappearance might be pertinent to the case." I must have snapped out the last few lines, based on Pat's expression and Kathleen's tone when she spoke again.

"Sorry. I'm under a time crunch right now. I didn't mean to give you a hard time. I'll have my people look for Carter, but right now, I'm running out of opportunities to keep my main suspects in town. I'm not even certain that I can convince them that they have to stay here overnight again. Without any real evidence against any of them, it's not going to take much to make me let them go for good, and if I allow that, I have a hunch that we're *never* going to solve the case."

"Do you really think one of them killed Bones?" I asked her.

"Well, I'm pretty sure that Timothy didn't do it, aren't you?"

"Of course I am," I said indignantly.

"Hey, take it easy, Annie. We're on the same team, remember?"

"Sorry. Now it's my turn to apologize. Carter could have done it," I suggested.

"I admit that the fact that he's running away isn't a good sign. It could mean that Bones found the money, Carter saw it happen, and he confronted him on the spot. They argued, Carter killed him, and then he stole the money. Why *wouldn't* he run, with that kind of pressure on him?"

"There's another scenario," I said.

"I'm listening."

"What if he saw the real killer murder Bones and steal the money? He could have been found out somehow, and now he's worried that the murderer is going to come after him next."

"It's a possibility," Kathleen said. "Either way, we need to find him before anyone else does. In the meantime, I'm going to try to sweat these four kids one last time and see if I can break one of them. It's not the most elegant police work I've ever done, but I'm at the end of my rope. I've got them separated, and I'm rotating between rooms trying to make something happen."

"Meanwhile, we still don't know where Carter is."

"I'm working with limited manpower here, Annie. What else can I do?"

"Pat and I can look for him ourselves," I offered.

"No!"

"Kathleen, do you really have any choice? If we find him, we'll call you before we do anything else. What could that hurt?"

"I can't even begin to consider the possibilities," she said with a sigh. "Fine. But if you do get lucky and stumble across him, don't do anything until you've spoken to me first. Can you and your brother agree to at least that much?"

"I can speak for Pat when I say that you have our word."

He looked at me quizzically, but I didn't have time to explain what

I'd just bound him to. That would have to wait until Kathleen and I were through.

"Don't make me live to regret this, Annie," she said.

"Trust me. It will be fine."

"I hope so, but I'm not going to hold my breath."

After I hung up, Pat asked, "What did you just promise our big sister? Thanks for speaking for me without asking me first, by the way."

"I didn't have any choice. It was the only way she'd agree to let us look for Carter," I said.

"I'm still waiting to hear what you promised."

"We can look for him, but we can't speak with him until we talk to her first. That's not so bad, is it?"

"I guess not," Pat said. "Where do we look, though?"

"First, we need to give this place a more thorough search," I said as I looked around the small living quarters.

"That should take all of thirty seconds," Pat said. "What are we supposed to do after that?"

"One step at a time, little brother," I said with a grin.

We did a much more thorough job this time, and it took quite a bit more time than thirty seconds, but we didn't have any more luck than we had before. There just wasn't that much space to hide a clue in. Whatever might have been there at one point had clearly been removed. That gave me an idea.

"What now?" Pat asked me.

"There's just one thing left to do," I said as I headed for the door.

"Would you care to share your plan with me?"

"What choice do we have? There's only one option left. We have to go through his trash and see if he threw anything away that might tell us where he went and why."

CHAPTER 18: PAT

I'VE DONE WORSE THINGS IN my life than dig through someone else's trash, but it still wasn't my favorite thing to do. Annie didn't seem to mind as we went down the stairs and started pawing through a black trash bag sitting on top of the bin. I couldn't imagine what could be worth finding in Carter's discarded rubbish, but she was right; we at least owed it to ourselves to look.

I hadn't given it a second thought, but of course we must have looked like idiots out there sorting through debris at curbside. Beatrice Masterson came out in a paisley dress that covered most of her body. She looked quizzically at us as she approached. "May I help you two with something?"

"No thanks. We're just doing a little exploring," Annie said.

Beatrice looked flustered by the news. "Excuse me?"

It was time for me to explain exactly what it was we were doing. "We're looking for a clue that might tell us where Carter Hayes moved to," I said. "You don't happen to know, do you?"

"Carter moved? When? I just saw him yesterday, for goodness sakes. That's nonsense."

"I'm afraid that it's true enough. Didn't he say anything to you about it?" I asked her.

"No, and I refuse to believe it's true," Beatrice said as she hurried past us and up the stairs. Annie and I had no choice but to follow her. The landlady stepped inside, and after a moment's search, she said, "That's impossible."

"Why is that?" I asked her.

"There is no way on earth that Carter would leave without telling me."

"Are you two really that close?" Annie asked her.

"Hardly. I rent this place to respectable tenants, but I don't have a relationship with them."

"Then why are you so surprised that he left without giving you any notice?" I asked.

"You know Carter. Do you honestly think that he'd leave willingly, given the fact that I insisted upon a five hundred dollar security deposit when he moved in?"

Beatrice had a point. It was common knowledge that Carter believed in squeezing every penny until it cried out in pain more than any other credo, and the idea that he'd leave good money behind in any case but the direst emergency was unfathomable.

"Where could he have gone, then?" Annie asked her.

The landlady frowned a few moments in thought. "He's estranged from his family—over money, of course—and as far as I know, he has only one friend in all of Maple Crest."

"A name might be helpful," Annie said. I hadn't realized that Carter had *any* friends, and clearly, neither had my twin sister.

"Darrel Hodges," she said.

"What on earth does a sculptor have in common with a man like Carter Hayes?" I asked her. Darrel was an artist with any carving tool you could name and some of them you couldn't. Though his work had gained a national reputation, you'd never know it by talking to him. He was as humble now as he'd always been.

"You'd have to ask him that," Beatrice said. "Now, if you don't mind, I need to go back in the house and collect myself. This is most disturbing."

"We understand," Annie said.

As we followed Beatrice back down the stairs, she said, "I'll trust that you'll stop what you were doing immediately."

I wanted to oblige her, but I wasn't sure we were ready to give up a potential lead. Annie spoke up before I could, though. "I can understand why you might not be happy with us digging through your trash out here, but would you mind if we take it with us?"

Beatrice looked shocked by the very notion of it, but ultimately all she could manage was a shrug. "Just don't let anyone see you taking it. I'd hate for people to talk." It was clear by her demeanor that she thought my twin sister and I had both gone insane, and she didn't want anyone to associate our behavior with her.

"We'd be happy to take it away," Annie said.

"The bag on top is his. The rest of it is mine, and I'll thank you to leave it exactly where it is." Beatrice walked back inside without a glance toward us, no doubt already trying to disassociate herself from us.

"Can you believe that?" I asked Annie.

"I know. I thought for a second there she was going to have a stroke when I asked her if we could take Carter's trash with us."

"I'm not talking about that. I mean the idea that Carter and Darrel are friends," I said.

"You never know. Should we sort through the trash first, or should we go ask Darrel if he knows where Carter might be?"

"The trash can wait," I said. "Let's go see Darrel."

"All in all, I think that's a solid game plan," Annie said as she threw the garbage bag into the back of her pickup truck.

"Darrel, do you have a second?" I asked the sculptor as he finally put down the carving tool in his hands. We'd been standing in the courtyard of his studio watching him work for a good five minutes, afraid to interrupt his progress. A slab of walnut about five feet tall and a good foot in diameter was mounted on top of his workbench. All of the bark had been removed, and the face of it had been squared off to show the grain beneath. Within the confines of the wood, Darrel was creating waves and flames. It was amazing, even at this raw stage, and it was no wonder that his work had been featured all over the country.

"Hey guys. What's up?" he asked.

"Are we interrupting you?" Annie asked. "It's really beautiful."

"I beg to differ," the carver said as he motioned toward one of the confluences of fire and water. "I can't get this to look organic enough for my taste, and I'm at a loss as to how to fix it."

"If you don't like it, I'll gladly take it for my cabin," Annie said with a smile.

Darrel chuckled. "I'm nowhere near giving up on this, but if I do, it's going into the fire pit instead of someone's home. I tend to burn my mistakes so no one else can see them."

"You'd burn this?" I asked, appalled by the very thought of it. "You can't do that!"

"Nice to see your passion, Pat. I probably won't. This has potential if I don't muck it up. It's kind of disappointing, actually. When I begin, I normally see exactly what I want to create in my mind, but I never seem to manage to come even close in reality."

"I find that hard to believe," I said.

"I get it," Annie added.

He smiled at her before he spoke. "That's because you're an artist, too."

"Me? I couldn't draw a stick figure in the mud with my finger."

"There are more ways to commit art than what I do," Darrel said. "Your talents are more culinary in nature, but don't kid yourself; you're every bit as much an artist as I am."

"I think you've been out in the sun too long," she said with a smile, but I could see that my sister appreciated the comment.

"I need to step away from this for a few minutes to get a little perspective on it, so I'm free to chat. I know you two didn't come out here to admire my work in progress. What's up?"

"We're looking for Carter Hayes," I said. "Do you have any idea where he might be?"

Darrel frowned as he sharpened the tip of his carving tool absently. "Why would you ask me that?"

"We heard that you were friends," I said.

"Where did you hear that?"

It wasn't a denial, nor was it a ringing endorsement. "Is it true or not?" I asked him.

"I suppose you could label our relationship that way. Carter brings me interesting wood from time to time, and if I like it, I buy it from him. While he's here, we'll share a cup of coffee or tea and chat. Is that enough to qualify as a friendship? I've been pals with Jimmy Oleander since we were kids. That's what I really call a friend."

"We're concerned about Carter's well-being," Annie said.

I wasn't sure that was precisely the truth, but I could see why my sister would say it. If we told Darrel that Carter was a suspect in a murder, and possibly on the run to boot, the sculptor might not be as inclined to answer our questions.

"Why is that?" he asked, looking a little alarmed by my twin sister's statement.

"We believe that he might have gotten mixed up in something over his head," I said. "We wanted to talk to him, but apparently he's moved out of his apartment without a word to his landlady."

"I'll bet Beatrice had a fit," Darrel said with a grin.

"She told us that Carter didn't even collect his security deposit before he left," I said.

"Now that is serious," Darrel said as he put down the tool in his hands. His smile was gone.

"Have you seen him lately?"

"Sure. He came by this morning, but he didn't say anything to me about leaving town."

"Do you mind if we ask why he was here?" I asked him. "We don't want you to betray any trusts, but we'd really like to talk to him, so anything you might be able to tell us might help."

"I don't suppose it's any big secret," Darrel said. "I owed him a little money, and he came by to collect."

"How much was it?" I asked him.

Darrel frowned. "Pat, I like you and your sister, but I'm not sure that's any of your business. What are you two up to?" Before either one of us could answer, he nodded. "Never mind. You're digging into that college kid's murder, aren't you? That must have been terrible for you, Annie, finding him floating in your pond like that."

"I wasn't the one who found him," she clarified. "Is that what folks in town are saying?"

Darrel shrugged. "You know how the rumor mill runs. If the truth isn't spectacular enough, then a little embellishment is always welcome."

"I know that all too well from firsthand experience," Annie said. "Where would he go, Darrel?"

"I have no idea," the sculptor said as he frowned. "If he was bugging out, he didn't share any of the details with me."

"Thanks anyway. If he happens to come by, would you mind giving us a call?" I asked him.

"I'm not sure that I can do that," Darrel said.

"Why not? We don't mean him any harm," I answered.

"Whether you do or not, I'll have to ask him about it first," Darrel said.

"In answer to your earlier question, evidently it's yes."

"What are you talking about?" he asked me.

"Whether or not you two are friends. You just tried to protect him, so I'd say that you were more than just business acquaintances."

"I guess you're right," Darrel said as he studied the wood in front of him. "Maybe if I take this swoop and split it in two, I can go deeper with the flame within the wave. It's going to be tricky, but it just might work."

"Are you asking us for our opinions?" Annie asked him.

"What? No. No thanks. I was just thinking out loud. If you two will excuse me, I've got work to do." Without another word, he picked up his carving tool and got back to work. Within a few seconds, he was so focused on what he was doing that I doubted he'd even remember later that we were ever there.

"Well, that turned out to be a dead end," I said as Annie and I got back into her truck.

"You never know. Carter could show up later, and if he does, Darrel might call us."

"That's quite a lot to wish for, Annie," I said. "Do you honestly think he'll remember we were even there talking to him? The man has passion and focus that I really envy."

"I don't," Annie said. "He seems consumed by his art. I wonder if he ever manages to stop thinking about it."

"That's something you'd have to ask him. Where to now?"

"How about we go back to the Iron," she suggested as she started in that direction. "We can't exactly drive all over Maple Crest hoping to find Carter. Maybe there's something in his trash that will tell us where he might have gone."

"And why," I added.

"I thought we'd cleared that up before. He's either running away from committing a murder, or he's afraid that he's the next victim on the real killer's list."

"If I were Carter Hayes, I wouldn't be happy about either prospect," I said. "I'm glad I'm not in his shoes."

"For so many reasons," Annie said. "Let's get to work."

CHAPTER 19: ANNIE

As I drove my pickup truck back to the Iron, I couldn't keep from wondering where Carter could have gone. "Pat, I don't like the fact that he just cleared out like that. It sounds as though he has money, since Darrel admitted to paying him earlier, so whether he grabbed that treasure from Bones or not, he could be anywhere now."

"That's true, but let's consider what we know about the man," my brother said. "He's the true definition of a miser. Can you see him using *any* money he didn't have to spend on a bus ticket or even a hotel room? If he can get away with it, his time on the road isn't going to cost him a dime."

"Even if he's hiding from the law or a murderer? Wouldn't it be worth everything he had to save his own life?" I asked him.

"You know as well as I do that old habits are the hardest ones to break sometimes."

"Okay, even if that's true, where could he hide around here for free?"

"That's what I keep asking myself," Pat said. "Maybe we'll get a hint in his trash."

"I hope so, because we're running out of options, and Kathleen is nearly out of time. If those four kids leave town and go back to school, her chances of solving Bones's murder drop dramatically."

"Should we be focusing on the kids instead, then?" Pat asked. "If Carter really is missing, chances are good that he's going to stay that way. With those four kids, though, we know they'll be gone shortly. Maybe we should focus on them instead."

"I'd love to," I said as I pulled up to the Iron's parking lot. During regular business hours, I never parked so close to the front, but we were closed, and for what it was worth, it would be getting dark soon. I didn't relish walking very far to get to my truck, even with the glare of the lights out front casting shadows all around us. "I'm getting a little hungry. How about you?"

"I could eat," Pat admitted, "but shouldn't we go through the trash first?"

"That depends. Would you rather do it on a full stomach or an empty one?" I asked as I reached in back and pulled out the garbage bag.

"Empty," Pat said quickly. "That way we can wash up when we're through and concentrate on our food instead of the task ahead."

"Fine," I said as my brother unlocked the front door, walked inside, and then locked it back behind us. "Where should we do this?" I asked.

"How about out back?" Pat suggested.

"In the storeroom?"

"No, in the back near the fire pit," he said. After looking up into the sky, he said, "We still have a little light left."

I didn't relish having Carter's trash spread out inside the Iron myself, and I didn't even live there full time. "Sure. That works for me."

He looked relieved at my acceptance. Once we were out back, I opened the bag and spread its contents out on the ground carefully while Pat grabbed one of the big trash bins we kept there.

"What's that for?"

"As we eliminate items, we can put them here," he said.

"I like it. Does it have a fresh bag inside?"

"Skip changed it when we closed this afternoon," Pat said. "It should be empty."

Once we confirmed that it was, we started picking the parts of Carter's trash out of the pile that had no apparent significance to us. By using this process of elimination, I hoped that when we got down to the nitty gritty, we'd be able to find something, anything, that would help us track Carter Hayes down.

Once we'd examined and then discarded frozen pizza boxes, dirty paper plates, empty tissue boxes, and an assortment of other detritus of Carter's life, we were left with precious little. The only things remaining were a few wadded-up pieces of notebook paper, a section torn from our local phone book, and a clipping from the town newspaper. I studied them each in turn but realized that the light had faded faster than I'd thought it would. "Can we at least take this stuff inside?" I asked my brother. "I can barely read most of it."

"I don't see what it could hurt," Pat said as he put our remaining clues into another clean garbage bag. "I'm going to wash up in the outdoor sink before we go in, if you don't mind."

"Why would I mind? I'm right behind you," I said. We'd had the sink installed originally to help during my outdoor cast iron cooking classes, but it had proved to be handy in many other ways as well. After our hands had been thoroughly scrubbed, we walked back into the Iron to see whether we'd finally hit pay dirt or if this was just another dead end in a long line of failures.

"That was one colossal waste of time," I told Pat as we went through the final bits of paper we'd kept out of the trash. "Nothing in that mess was the least bit helpful."

"Annie, most of what we do in our investigations leads to dead ends," my brother reminded me. "It's not like the movies where the perfect clue shows up at precisely the right moment in time. We have to keep working to find anything we can use."

"In the meantime, where do we look next?" I asked him.

"Short of driving around Maple Crest searching for Carter, I think we have to focus on the suspects whose whereabouts we know."

"I'm not talking to Timothy about Bones's murder anymore," I said emphatically.

"I could do it myself," Pat offered.

"No!" I hadn't meant to be so forceful with him. In a gentler voice, I continued, "Pat, you could show me videotape of Timothy hitting Bones with that pickaxe and I still wouldn't believe it. If he did it, it's going to be up to Kathleen to prove it, because as far as I'm concerned, he's off our list of suspects, now and forever." I could see Pat frowning slightly, so I added, "Does it make sense to handle him that way? Of course not. Timothy had the opportunity, anybody near the site had the means with that tool lying around, and as to motive, anger and even greed works for just about everyone as well. Nevertheless, we're dropping Timothy's name from our list, and if you don't agree with me, then you can keep looking without me, brother or not."

Pat looked at me for a few seconds before he spoke again. "Are you finished? Did you get that all out of your system?"

I couldn't help myself. I grinned in spite of what I'd just said. "Yes, as a matter of fact, I feel much better now. That doesn't mean that I didn't mean everything that I just said. You know that, don't you?"

"I get it. I'm good with dropping him if you are. That still leaves us with five viable suspects, and our big sister happens to be monopolizing the four we need to speak with at the moment."

"Why don't I call her and see what's going on with them?" I suggested.

"What are you going to say? I have a feeling that Kathleen's not going to let us speak with any of them."

"I have the same feeling, but what could it hurt to try?" I dialed her number, and to my surprise, she picked up almost immediately.

"I was just about to call you," Kathleen said when she realized that I was on the other end.

"Why? Did you get a confession out of one of them?"

"Hardly," Kathleen said, and I could hear the defeat in her tone of voice. "I was hoping you and Pat had been able to come up with something I could use, because frankly, I'm all tapped out."

"We still can't find Carter, Timothy has been exonerated for no other reason than he's my boyfriend, and we can't do anything else without talking to your four students."

"They aren't my students, at least not much longer," Kathleen said. "Marty is making noises saying that I can't keep any of them much longer, and he's right. Sometimes I curse the Internet. It makes everyone believe they are experts in the law."

I felt a sinking feeling in the pit of my stomach. "Did you already let them go?"

"No, but it's going to happen soon enough. The only reason I've been able to stall them this long is by lying to them, something you know that I hate to do."

"What did you tell them?" I asked her. Kathleen was a stickler when it came to the truth.

"I said that Ginny Bost had the key to the evidence locker where their driver's licenses are being held, and she won't be back in town until morning. They bought it, so then I had to send Ginny away with the key so that technically, I wasn't lying to them. She didn't mind, but it makes my crew even lighter. If I were a criminal, right now would be the perfect time to commit a crime wave in Maple Crest."

"Let's just keep that to ourselves, then, shall we?" I asked her. "Are you housing them at the police station again tonight?"

"No, they've already told me that they won't stand for that again," Kathleen said.

"We made the offer before, but I'm willing to make it again. Pat and I could take them tonight, and while they're with us, we can press them a little harder," I offered.

"I doubt they'd be any more tempted to sleep on the floor of your store than they would be staying with me at the station."

I had a sudden thought. "They don't have to. You could bring them all out to my cabin. They'll love it out there, compared to their other choices."

"Annie, I'm still not keen about you and Pat being alone with them out there in the middle of nowhere, and you know it."

"You could always come, too," I offered.

"Where would I sleep, under the stars? There's not enough room for six people as it is, and besides, I'm not their favorite person on the planet at the moment."

"Don't worry about it. We'll make it work," I said. "I'll even feed them. If you present it in the right way, they might even be eager to come out to my place. We can have a fire, and I'll even cook something in my Dutch oven over the coals. What do you have to lose at this point?"

"I hate to admit it, but you're right. I need to do *something* before I let them waltz out of town like a murder was nothing. Are you sure that you and Pat are up to this?"

"We'll be fine," I said, volunteering my brother yet again for something dangerous. It was a safe thing to offer; I knew that he'd have my back, regardless of the level of danger we might be putting ourselves in.

"I don't suppose I have any choice. Let me ask them, and then I'll get back to you."

"Thanks, Kathleen."

"You're even crazier than you seem thanking me for this. I'm putting both of you in jeopardy, Annie, and you know it."

"No worries," I said. "Besides, you're just a phone call away if we happen to stumble across any clues."

"Don't you forget it, either," she said.

After she hung up, Pat asked, "What did she say? Did she go for it?"

"You heard enough of that from my end of the conversation to put all of that together?" I asked him in amazement.

"I think so. You're proposing that we have a slumber party at the cabin, you're going to cook outside on an open fire, and then we're all bunking inside in sleeping bags. By morning's light, with any luck, we'll have the killer isolated, and then the rest of us all live happily ever after. What could possibly go wrong with a plan like that?" he asked me with a broad grin.

"When you put it that way, I have to admit that it does sound a little insane," I said as I started scrounging in the freezer for something to make for our meal later.

"If you can think of a way to say it that it doesn't sound reckless, I'd love to hear it," Pat said.

"Hush and get some vegetables together. We've got a big meal to prep."

"I'll do it after I get a snack first," he said. "I'm hungry right now, and it appears I'm going to have to wait a bit before I get my supper."

CHAPTER 20: PAT

As Annie drove us to her cabin in the woods in her pickup truck, I still didn't feel any easier about our plan. There were so many things that could go wrong with it, and very few that could turn out right, that I decided that the best thing I could do was not to think of it at all. We'd be ad libbing a lot, and most times I preferred a solid plan. As things stood, we had to dance a pretty fine line between being too aggressive with our questioning and being too timid. We'd either alienate all of them, or they'd leave in the morning without us learning a thing that might help our investigation.

"What's our plan again?" I asked Annie as we neared her driveway.

"We need to get them to open up to us," she said as she suddenly veered her pickup off the road and up a narrow grass lane that looked all too familiar.

"Why are we going back to the crime scene?" I asked her as we bounced up the narrow path.

"Didn't you spot it? The tape has been torn down," she said as she pointed to one edge, tethered to a tree on one end, while the other end fluttered in the breeze.

"Kathleen could have released the land," I suggested.

"Without taking the crime scene tape with her? Seriously?"

Annie was right. That didn't sound like our big sister at all. Kathleen wouldn't sleep in a bed that was unmade, she was so precise about her life. Leaving something as significant as crime scene tape behind was completely out of character for her, and I knew that her officers would have collected it themselves for fear of our big sister's wrath.

"Somebody's back here, then," I suggested.

"That's what I want to find out," Annie said as she slowed her progress for a large ditch that crossed the path.

"Shouldn't we go back to the main road, call Kathleen, and see what she has to say?"

My twin sister shook her head. "What if it's nothing? Do you really want to give her a reason to change her mind about allowing our little slumber party tonight? I have a hunch she's just looking for a reason to cancel it."

"Why should that matter?" I asked.

"It shouldn't, but you weren't the one who talked to her. She was on the edge about allowing us to do this. If we give her the slightest reason to back out, she's going to do it. I guarantee it."

"Fine," I said, finding it hard to argue with my sister's logic. "Just take it easy, okay?"

"Relax. There's only one way in or out of the dig site, and it's down this road."

"You call this a road?" I asked her as she hit another bump and sent me flying upward.

"It will do until something better comes along," Annie said, the grim determination evident on her face.

"You don't happen to be armed, do you?" I asked her.

"No. How about you?"

"No, ma'am. Do you at least have a tire iron or something stout like that banging around in the bed of your truck?"

"I took it out two days ago," she admitted.

"To change a flat tire?"

"No, I grabbed it to use as a weapon myself, and then I forgot it on my front porch."

"So, we're defenseless," I said.

"Not as long as I've got this," she said, patting the dashboard. "This pickup will protect us. Just wait and see."

"Hopefully it won't come to that," I said.

"You worry too much, Pat," Annie told me as we rounded another corner, getting closer and closer to the site where the students had been digging.

"Somebody has to balance out the fact that you don't worry nearly enough," I said with a weak smile. "Can you at least pull over so I can find a tree branch or something?"

"Too late. We're here," she said, and with that, with one more turn, we were back to the murder scene.

"What are you hoping to find?" I asked my twin as we looked around the empty clearing.

"I don't know," she said. "Is there anything we might have missed before?"

We both got out of the truck and started walking around the site. While Annie studied the holes that had already been dug, I looked at the old stone foundation where a house had once stood. How had they managed to carve a home out of the woods so long ago using nothing but the natural resources around them? If the same task were to be put to me to achieve today, I was fairly certain that I would die of exposure, starvation, or predators, whichever finished me off first. Then I looked at the small cemetery and realized that the life expectancy back then was nothing to brag about, either. All of the remaining tombstones were hand-carved stone, the wooden ones having rotted and faded into the ground long before. The names read like a history book, full of birth and death dates far too close together. There were plenty of Blankenships represented, but there were other names as well. Harding, Bless, Davidson, Cash, Jenkins, and Parsons were contributors, too. How many deaths had this land seen over the centuries?

"Pat, why are you standing there reading tombstones?" Annie asked me as she approached.

"I'm not quite sure. They just caught my eye for some reason."

"What we need to find is something a little bit more recent," Annie replied. She walked several yards to the tight circle of rocks that had to be where the well had once been, supplying all of the water the homestead had needed. The opening was now covered by a mossy board lying across its top. "Do you think there's any water still down there now?" she asked.

"I have no idea," I said.

"Let's check and see," Annie answered as she started to lift up the homemade lid.

"Do you honestly think anyone would hide their money down there?" I asked her.

"It's not as crazy as it sounds," Annie answered. "I've been reading up on old homesteaders, and I discovered that they liked to keep their wealth close by. Why should Jasper Blankenship be any different?"

"When have you had time to read up on anything like that?"

"I had trouble sleeping last night," she admitted as we pried off the top together. It had been there so long that the grass and weeds had grown up around three edges of the board, making it difficult to dislodge it without a pry bar. "I finally gave up trying, so I started doing some Internet searches. It's really pretty fascinating."

"I bet," I said. "Did you happen to stumble across anything more specific than that?" I asked as we finally managed to free the lid.

"One source said that common hiding places were in the basement, in and around the well, near big trees that served as landmarks, or places like old gardens, cemeteries, even their barns."

"I'll take your word for it," I said as I looked down into the pit. It wasn't very deep; in fact, it appeared that at some point in the distant past, someone had filled a great deal of it up with rocks and other debris. "There's nothing here."

Annie looked over the edge with me. "Not that we can see, at least. Why would anyone ever fill in a well? Could Jasper's treasure be down there?"

"More likely it went dry at some point, and they filled it in to keep their kids from falling down into an empty hole," I said as I put the cover back in place. "It sounds as though there are too many places to look in such a limited amount of time, and I doubt Timothy would appreciate us being here, let alone taking a shovel to his land."

"We're not digging up anything," Annie said. "I just think the college expedition may have been a little too restricted in their search before."

"Be sure to tell them all that tonight," I said with a grin. "I'm sure they'd be delighted to get your constructive criticism."

My sister stuck her tongue out at me, something that never failed to make me chuckle.

"If we're not going to do any digging, then why are we here?" I asked her.

"We're looking for something like this," she said as she squatted down near the old foundation of the homestead. It was on the back, well away from the clearing, and I wondered if Kathleen's people had even searched there. I joined my sister and looked at the spot she was checking out.

"What do you think, Pat?"

"It's just another hole, as far as I can see," I said.

"It's more than that," Annie replied as she reached down into the gash in the earth and pulled her soiled hand away. "Check it out, Pat. It's fresh."

"Are you sure?" I asked her as I got a closer look for myself.

She pointed to a circle of grass that had recently been uprooted and was lying off to one side. "Look, the blades are still green. Now check out where they dug the day before."

I looked over at the closest other hole and saw that she was right. The grass that had been removed the day before was already browning at the tips, whereas this bit seemed just as lively as the grass that surrounded us. "I see what you mean."

"Who was out here digging today?" she asked. "They had to go through the police tape to get here, so it's obvious they were ignoring Kathleen's warning not to cross the line."

"I know you're not going to be happy about what I'm about to say, but Timothy could have done it, Annie."

She looked long and hard at me before she answered. "You heard me before, Pat. He's off the table as far as a suspect for murder is concerned."

"Even if he dug this hole, it doesn't necessarily mean that he's a killer," I said quickly before my sister could build up a head of steam.

"Why do you say that?"

"If we're right, and Bones found at least part of the money that was buried out here, why would anyone dig over here?" I pointed to the spot a hundred yards away where Peggy had claimed to have discovered the college student's body. "Doesn't it just make sense that if someone killed him for gold and silver, they'd keep looking for more where they found him in the first place? This is an entirely different dig site over here."

"Okay, I see what you're saying. That implies that whoever dug this fresh hole *isn't* the killer, since they wouldn't know where Bones was actually murdered."

"Or even spoke with Peggy," I added. "That would make me believe that it had to be Timothy or Carter. Do you think there's one chance in a hundred that Peggy hasn't already recounted every gruesome detail of her discovery to the people she's here with? If one of them came back to investigate on their own, they'd dig over there."

"Even if the killer wasn't one of them, they'd do the same thing," Annie said.

"I don't follow."

"What if whoever killed Bones only got part of the loot, as you just suggested? They might sneak back looking for the rest of it, but they wouldn't be searching over here, either."

"There's something else we haven't considered," I told her.

"What's that?"

"The four students have been with Kathleen most of the day, and I have a hunch that if they haven't, they've at least all been together. When could one of them have had the time it must have taken to break free from the group, come back here, and start digging again?"

"We'll have to ask them that tonight at dinner," Annie suggested. "In the meantime, let's assume that it wasn't one of the four of them. That leaves Carter." She looked hard at me again, daring me to bring up Timothy's name again. I wasn't about to say it, even though I felt that this time, it would be a good thing. At the very least, it would imply that her boyfriend hadn't had anything to do with Bones's murder, and as far as my twin sister was concerned, that should offer her welcome relief from the direst of the possibilities we'd been considering.

"So we can assume that Carter didn't kill Bones, but he's looking for the gold and silver coins nonetheless," I said.

"And if that's true, it means Timothy has a right to be upset with him, but it clears Carter Hayes of murder."

"Based on that line of reasoning, it also means that Carter left his apartment because he was afraid for his life, which leads us back to Marty, Gretchen, Peggy, and Henry."

"Then it's a good thing that we're going to have complete access to the four of them until morning," Annie said. "We just have to make sure that we make our time with them count."

"Then we should get busy at your place, shouldn't we?" I asked her.

"Yes, but I want to get a few shots of this first with my camera phone. You could make yourself useful and take a few photographs of some of the other landmarks around us while you're waiting on me."

"Why would I want to do that?" I asked her.

"Because we never know what's going to be useful to us or not."

I shrugged, took a few shots of the covered well, and then snapped a few random images of the headstones just for fun.

"Are you ready?" Annie asked me just as I took another photograph.

"Yes," I said as I put my own phone away. "I don't think whoever dug that fresh hole found anything."

"Why do you say that?"

"I don't believe they had time to," I said. "That hole wasn't nearly as neat as the others were. I have a feeling that we interrupted someone before they could find what they were looking for."

Annie still hadn't put her phone away. As she dialed a number, I asked her, "Are you calling Kathleen after all?"

"She needs to get someone out here," Annie said. "Even if this isn't related to Bones's murder, no one should be out here."

"Even Timothy?" I took a chance of suggesting.

"Even him," she said.

A minute later, she hit something on her phone and put it back into her pocket.

"No luck?" I asked her.

"It went straight to voicemail. I'll just tell her when she brings the troops out to my place."

I glanced at my watch. "Which is going to happen sooner rather than later. Shouldn't we get going?"

"Yes, but I'd still like to snoop around here a little more," Annie said. "I've got a hunch this land has more secrets to give up if we're just smart enough to find them."

"According to some old stories I've heard, folks have been looking for Jasper's treasure for a great many years. A few days shouldn't matter much, one way or the other."

"I'm not talking about treasure hunting," Annie said a little too severely. "I'm looking for the killer."

"And I'm not?" I asked her sharply.

She frowned, and then it slowly transformed itself into the hint of a smile. "I'm sorry, Pat. You're right. I get carried away sometimes."

"You don't have to tell me that," I said, smiling in return, showing her that all was well between us.

"Let's get going," Annie said.

As we got into the truck, I asked, "Is there anything I can do to help when we get to the cabin?"

"You can start a fire," she said.

"It's not that chilly yet," I replied as she carefully turned around and drove back down the path we'd come up so recently.

"Maybe not, but it will be later this evening. Besides, this fire isn't going to be strictly for warmth. I've decided that my cabin's going to be crowded enough when we all finally go to sleep tonight, so I'm going to use the great outdoors as our kitchen, dining room, and living room this evening."

"That sounds like a good plan to me," I said. "In answer to your question, I'd be delighted to start the fire."

"Of course you would," she said, grinning. "Has a man been born yet that wasn't a pyromaniac the second he popped out of his mother's womb?"

"Maybe so, but if there is, I haven't met him yet, and I'm not sure that I'd like to. Fire brings out the primitive side of our nature. There's something elemental about it that I can't explain, but I know its pull when I feel it."

"Timothy acts the exact same way," she said, and I could see a hint of sadness in her gaze as she spoke. It would be difficult for her to mend fences with him after this was over, but if anyone could do it, I knew that Annie could. At least I had been spared that much. Jenna was still out of town, and one way or the other, by the time she got back to Maple Crest, our investigation would be finished. I couldn't imagine the circumstances that would keep our four main suspects in town after the next morning, so Annie and I had to work quickly. There had to be a way of figuring out who the killer was.

I just wished we had a single clue as to how to go about it.

At least we had some time alone with our suspects, which may not have been the best thing for our prospects of achieving long-term health. After all, the odds were pretty good that one of them was a killer, and we were about to enter into a situation when our very lives were going to hang in the balance. If we got too close, the murderer might consider us threats that had to be eliminated. On the other hand, if we missed this opportunity to figure out exactly who had done it, we'd never get another chance.

Either way, I had the feeling that Annie and I were in for a long night.

Just how long, I had no idea at that moment, but I would find out soon enough.

CHAPTER 21: ANNIE

WHILE PAT STARTED WORKING ON getting the fire started in the pit out by the pond, I went inside to prep the night's meal. At least I knew that none of our guests were vegetarians, since they'd all eaten at my grill before. That was a real plus, since nearly all of my cast iron meals tended to be meat centric. It wasn't that I couldn't make anything without including meat in it; it just wasn't my preference. The evening's meal was going to be a fairly standard stew, one that I would feel comfortable serving to just about anyone. Since my exterior Dutch oven had three legs to keep it elevated above the coals, I tended to brown my meat inside when the opportunity presented itself with one of my standard skillets at the stovetop. That would come later, though. Once I had everything set up inside, I walked outside to see how the fire was coming along.

"That looks great," I said as I joined Pat. He had a decent fire going, and I could already see some coals starting to form.

"I expected Kathleen to be here by now," he said.

"Should I call her?" I offered as he added a few more medium-sized logs to the fire.

"No, let's use the time we've got to figure out what we're going to do," he said.

"I thought we'd already decided on a game plan. First we feed them, then we entertain them, and just before bed, we pounce."

He laughed. "I was thinking we'd try something more subtle than that."

"What did you have in mind? Are we going to play good cop/bad cop? I'll do it, but only if I get to be the bad one."

"I was thinking more along the lines of us sowing doubt in everyone's minds about their compatriots. If we can get them to turn on each other, we might just see a crack in someone's armor."

"Do you think that could work?" I asked him.

"It's better than grilling them again. Kathleen's already exhausted that routine, so I feel as though we need to plant a little doubt and then step back and see what happens when they start dealing with their own issues without outside interference."

"When did you get so devious?" I asked my brother with a smile.

"It's what naturally happens when you grow up with two devious sisters," he answered with a chuckle.

"I'm going to take that as a compliment," I said.

"Good, because that's how I meant it."

Pat poked at the fire as I heard someone driving up my lane. That was one of the good things about living at the end of a pretty extensive driveway. Nobody could sneak up on me there, at least not on four wheels. Kathleen came around the corner in the police van, carrying our overnight guests, a group that just happened to include all of our most viable suspects.

"Thanks for doing this, Annie," Kathleen said loudly. "Everyone was happy to take you up on your generous offer."

"Not everybody," Marty said. "I still can't believe that your deputy left town with the keys to the lockup where our IDs and wallets were stored. What kind of Mayberry nightmare kind of town do you live in here?"

I could see Kathleen wasn't pleased with the criticism, but she did her best to smile. "As I said before, I apologize for any inconvenience this may be causing any of you. You have Maple Crest's most sincere regrets that this occurred."

"The only thing I regret is coming here in the first place," Marty said.

"You didn't have to, you know," Peggy said a little defensively. "We'd have been perfectly fine with just Henry to interpret the map he found."

Henry didn't comment, but I could see that he was trying to hide a smile and failing pretty miserably at it.

"Peggy, Marty's important, too," Gretchen said, coming to his defense, which definitely got the surly man's attention.

"Thanks," he said. "It's good to know that at least someone appreciates me."

Henry shook his head. "Marty, Peggy knows as well as I do that you've pitched in more than your share. Right, Peggy?" he asked as he turned to her.

"Of course," she said without making eye contact with Marty. It was clear to everyone there that her apology was less than sincere, but evidently Marty decided to ignore that fact.

"I thought we'd be eating soon," Peggy said as she looked at the fire. "Is it inside?"

"I haven't started cooking yet," I told them. "We have to let the fire die down more before the coals will be ready."

"I'm hungry now, though," she said.

"We could always start with dessert," I said. I'd snagged an apple pie when we'd left the Iron, figuring that it might make a nice ending for our meal.

"I'm all for that," Henry said.

"Sounds good to me, too," Peggy added, and the rest of the group nodded in agreement.

"Stay right here, and I'll grab the pie and plates," I said.

"Do you need a hand?" Peggy asked.

"Sure. That would be great."

"I'll help, too," Gretchen added.

"Thanks, but we've got it," I said. I wanted to get Peggy alone. Otherwise, it would be hard to plant any doubt in her mind about her companions. Gretchen looked disappointed, so I added, "You can help me with the meal prep later if you'd like."

"Cool," she said.

Kathleen looked at me steadily before she said, "If you'll all excuse me, I'd better get going. I've got rounds to make this evening."

"Will you be coming back by the cabin tonight?" Pat asked her.

"It's doubtful," she said, something that we'd arranged with her earlier. We wanted this group to be relaxed and confident that it would just be the six of us, without any signs of law enforcement there, even if it was our sister. Kathleen would come back later, but only if we called her. Otherwise, she was going to set up camp at the end of our driveway, just a minute away if things got ugly at some point and we needed her. She'd kept a sleeping bag for herself in the police van, and though Pat and I had argued with her about the arrangements, she'd insisted.

After Kathleen was gone, supposedly for the night, I said, "Let's go, Peggy."

We walked into my cabin, and I started gathering plates and forks.

"What can I do to help?" she asked me.

"You can grab the pie," I said. "I cut it earlier, so we should be fine." Pretending to just realize that we needed something else to drink so I could stall for a little time, I asked, "Does everyone in your group like coffee?"

"Oh, yes," she said.

"Then let's make some," I volunteered. "It won't take long."

Without even waiting for her to agree, I started a fresh pot. At least that way, I'd have a little time to talk to one of our lead suspects. After all, Pat and I had already realized that Peggy could have killed Bones and then reported finding his body on the dig site. But I knew that questioning her about that would get me nowhere. This situation called for a little more subtlety than that. "Henry seems to be quite a fan of yours," I said. "Have you two been dating long?"

She flushed a little before she replied, "Oh, we're not going out."

"But you'd like to, am I right?" I asked her.

"Let's just put it this way. If he asked me out, I wouldn't say no."

"Why would you? He's a nice-looking young man, and he seems

sweet as well. You should have seen him with Gretchen while you were in the hospital. He was really nice to her, too."

"What? He was with Gretchen?" Peggy asked, clearly alarmed by the prospect.

"They were both concerned about you," I said. "I think it helped them bond a little."

"But she likes Marty," Peggy protested.

"I'm sure you're right," I said, doing my best to sound as unconvincing as I could. "How did you get along with Bones?"

"He was all right," Peggy said.

"No sparks there, though?" I asked her.

"Romantically? No. Ewww."

"How about on his end?" I asked.

She hesitated too long before replying. "Not really."

"Peggy, that's not what I heard earlier. It was quite a bit more intense than that, wasn't it?" It was a shot worth taking, and I was pleased to see that it hit home.

She frowned for a moment, and then she started to cry. "He said he wouldn't say anything. I can't believe that he told you about it."

"Wouldn't you feel better if you told me about it yourself?" I asked her, since I had no idea what she was talking about.

"I thought Henry must have told you about it," she said, puzzled.

"No, he didn't breathe a word of it to me," I answered.

"It was really no big deal. Bones thought everyone was away from the main dig site, so he tried to make a move on me. I shut him down, but he had a hard time getting the message. I don't know what would have happened if Henry hadn't come back for some water. He saw what was going on, and he warned Bones that if he tried anything else, he'd have to answer to him. It was really kind of gallant when you think about it."

"So, Henry was jealous of the way Bones was acting? Is that what you're saying? Did it make him angry to see him pressing you?"

"It wasn't like that, Annie. He was just looking out for me, that's all."

I could see that I'd pushed her as far as I could manage. "I didn't mean to stir anything up. Would you mind taking the pie and the plates outside to the picnic table? You can send Gretchen in for the mugs, the napkins, and the forks."

"Okay," she said, but then she hesitated at the door. "Don't say anything to the others about what happened, okay? I don't want anyone else getting the wrong idea."

"What might that be?" I asked her.

"Henry was just trying to help me out, but I was perfectly capable of shutting Bones down by myself. I'd rather not talk about it anymore, if it's all the same to you."

"Got it," I said with a smile.

Peggy left, and as I waited for Gretchen to show up, I wondered about a new set of possibilities. Could Henry have killed Bones trying to protect Peggy? Or had she led me to that conclusion to draw suspicion away from herself? Then again, it might not be true at all, since she'd asked me not to say anything to the rest of the group about Bones's alleged behavior. I wondered if Henry would have a different story entirely if I managed to corner him and ask him about it myself. I was still trying to figure out if I'd actually learned anything useful at all when Gretchen came in.

"Peggy said you needed a hand," she said.

"If you'd hang back until the coffee is ready, you can take the tray out. That way you don't have to help me prep our dinner."

"I really don't mind," she said.

"I appreciate that, but I've been doing this for so long, I could just about cook with cast iron in my sleep. What's going on with you and Marty?"

"What do you mean?"

"You jumped to his defense pretty fast a few minutes ago," I said. "Is there something between you two, or are you just going after Henry?"

Gretchen shook her head. "I'm not interested in either one of them," she said.

"So, was it Bones you liked?" I was trying to drive some wedges in, but so far, at least with Gretchen, I wasn't having any luck.

"Bones? No. No way. He wasn't a very nice guy, to be honest with you."

"Did he make a hard pass at you, too?" I asked before I realized that I'd just told her something Peggy had asked me to keep in confidence. In my defense, I hadn't meant to do it, if that counted for anything, which I suspected it wouldn't, at least with Peggy.

Gretchen surprised me with her response. "He hit on Peggy, too? I know you shouldn't speak ill of the dead and all, but come on. That's just crazy."

"So, I take it you didn't reciprocate his affection."

"No. All Bones had going for him was his daddy's money. He was determined to find the Blankenship money and lord it over his father after we found it."

"Do you think he would have shared it with the rest of you if he'd found it first?" I asked.

Gretchen frowned. "I asked Marty that same question a few days ago. He assured me that it wasn't going to happen, so I shouldn't worry about it."

"How could he promise you something like that?" I asked her.

"He said he was keeping an eye on our team leader, so if anything untoward happened, he'd know about it."

"Does that mean that he saw Bones make a pass at you? He likes you, you know."

"I'm sure that it's nothing," Gretchen said.

"Maybe not as far as you're concerned, but I'm fairly certain that he has strong feelings for you."

"If he does, then I'll set him straight, just like I did Bones. I just got out of a long relationship. I'm not looking for anybody at the moment."

"Just treasure, right?"

Gretchen frowned. "Annie, I don't have a trust fund like Bones did or rich parents like Peggy and Henry must. I'm working my way through school. If we found something, I was going to use my share to pay off my student loans."

"What were the others going to do with their shares?" I asked her.

"Henry was going to use his portion to feed his research on other buried treasure. He believes he has a lead on where some of the lost Confederate gold disappeared to. Do you know about that?"

"It's hard not to, living around here. Most folks believe the treasure was found and spent a long time ago."

"Not Henry. He claims that he has a new lead from reading some personal histories of the gold shipment's escorts, and with some funding, he's sure he can find it."

"Why didn't he get Bones to finance it?" I asked.

Gretchen frowned. "He tried to, but Bones said that we had to find a smaller stake first, and then he'd consider it." She leaned forward as she added, "If we found anything here in Maple Crest, Henry wasn't going to let Bones in on the new excavation at all. Finding the Blankenship treasure is as important to his dreams as mine are to me." She glanced over at the coffee pot. "Is that ready yet?"

"It is," I said reluctantly. I wasn't finished talking with Gretchen, but my coffee pot had other ideas.

"I'll just take this out to everyone else. Are you coming, too?"

"Let me prep the meal, and I'll be right out. Does your offer to help still stand?" I was going to do whatever I could to get her to linger a little longer so we could chat a little more.

"I would be glad to help, but from the sound of things, I'd probably just get in your way," she said.

After Gretchen was gone, I decided to prep the meal as quickly as I could so I wouldn't miss anything outside. Adding a few tablespoons of olive oil and butter to one of my larger cast iron skillets, I put it on a burner and set it to medium heat. While the oil and butter were heating up, I took the stew beef I'd taken from the Iron and coated it in flour, lightly enhanced with salt and pepper. After they were prepped, I browned the chunks of beef in the skillet, and once they were finished on all sides, I transferred them to my Dutch oven. While the beef had been browning, I'd added a can of beef stock, two sliced onions, four cubed potatoes, six carrots cut into broad chunks, and a green pepper thrown in for good measure. At the last second, I added a few bay leaves and a bit of minced garlic, and it was ready for the fire once the meat had been added.

Grabbing my Dutch oven, now even heavier loaded with food nearly to the lid, I walked outside.

We were dealing with a limited amount of time now, and so far, my prodding hadn't produced much that we could use.

It was time to turn up the heat, in every way possible.

CHAPTER 22: PAT

"**H**ow do those coals look to you?" I asked Annie as she rejoined us outside. The cast iron was clearly heavy, but I knew better than to offer to carry it for her. My twin sister was a proud young woman, and I wasn't about to make her look the slightest bit weak with this crowd.

"They're perfect," she said as she put the pot down, and then, grabbing a nearby shovel, she started moving some of the glowing coals around. Once she had a nice little bed away from the main fire, she placed her covered Dutch oven down in the middle of it and then immediately added even more coals to the top of it. After Annie had it sitting comfortably on the fire, with a healthy amount of coals on top as well, it was time to push our guests a little harder.

Before I could do that, though, one of them spoke up first.

"Won't it burn everything on the inside with so many coals on top?" Henry asked.

"Heat rises, so I need more of it on top than I do on the bottom," Annie said. Holding her hand over the top, after a few moments she added, "That's running somewhere around 350 degrees F, so we should be fine."

"You're kidding, right?" Marty asked.

"About what?"

"How can you possibly know what the temperature is just using your hand?"

"I have no doubt she can do it," Gretchen said in my sister's defense. "After all, she's experienced in this type of cooking, and besides, it's still got to be a somewhat accurate way to measure the heat. How do you think a thermometer works?"

"With mercury?" he asked her.

"By heat radiation," Gretchen said.

"Thanks for having my back," Annie told her.

"I'm not taking sides. After all, it's just science."

Once the stew was going, I looked at the remaining firewood and realized that we didn't have enough wood to finish cooking our meal, let alone build the fire back up to a bonfire tonight so we could all spend some time together. Annie and I couldn't afford having everyone going to bed before we had a chance to throw some doubt into the group and then watch them react. I had a hunch that my sister had already spoken with Peggy and Gretchen while she'd had them isolated inside the cabin. Now it was my turn with the men. "Marty, would you help me with some firewood?"

"I'll do it," Henry said. "Marty isn't exactly the volunteering type."

"Why should I do it if I don't have to?" Marty replied, and then he turned to me. "Go on, Henry. Don't let me stop you from being a hero."

"Where's this wood?" Henry asked.

"It's at the back of the cabin," I said.

Henry pointed to some stacked much closer, still in earshot of the others. "What's wrong with that wood over there?"

"It's for a different sort of fire," Annie said when it was clear that I was at a loss for a response that sounded even vaguely plausible.

"Okay. Fine. Whatever."

"I guess I can help, too," Marty said after getting a dirty look from Gretchen.

I was still trying to figure out how to kill that particular suggestion when once again Annie came to my rescue. "Marty, you can help him with the next load. In the meantime, would you mind giving me a hand rearranging the fire? We don't want one side of the oven to get too hot."

"Let's go, Henry," I said before Marty could protest.

As we walked to the back of Annie's cabin, I asked him, "I can't seem to stop thinking about it. Do you have any idea who might have wanted to kill Bones?"

The historian frowned a moment before he spoke. "He wasn't the easiest guy in the world to get along with, but murder? No, I can't even imagine the circumstances that would drive someone to do that."

"Greed can be a pretty powerful factor," I said. "If he found some of the treasure, that might be motive enough."

"I guess. The whole world seems to be in debt these days, though. Why kill someone just to get ahead? It doesn't make any sense to me."

"Are you doing that well with your education expenses?"

"My parents are paying for most of it, but I've got a few loans, just like the rest of the student body at my school," he said. "It's nothing I can't handle."

"What are the prospects as a history major?" I asked him.

"Now you sound just like my folks," Henry said with a grin. "I'm not planning on teaching, if that's what you're asking. I've never been a big fan of working for other people. When I graduate, I've got a few ideas of my own. After all, there's more to history than what's in the textbooks."

"Are you going after more treasure?"

Henry looked at me oddly, and I knew that I'd made a good guess. It hadn't been that big a stretch. After all, this team had been assembled because of something Henry had found in an old journal. Maybe he had other leads as well. "This was supposed to finance the next hunt," he admitted. "I'm not sure what I'm going to do now. I suppose I'll go back to school tomorrow with the others and try to forget this ever happened. This is my last semester, so after this, I'll probably never see any of the rest of them again."

"Not even Peggy?" I asked him as we got to the far woodpile.

"You saw that, did you?" Henry asked with a smile.

"It's not hard to spot," I said.

"Pat, has there ever been a girl in your life that you tried to make something happen with, but it just wouldn't?"

"More than I can count on one hand," I said, laughing slightly.

"That's the story of my life. I like Peggy, and I think she likes me, too, but with this murder, any chance we had once is gone."

"Why do you say that?"

"It's pretty simple. How can we look at each other across a dinner table wondering if the other one is a cold-blooded killer? It's not exactly a recipe for a long-term relationship, you know?"

"I suppose not," I said.

"What's that sitting there for?" Henry asked me as he pointed to a nearby gasoline can. "Is that how Annie usually starts her fires?"

"Only in a pinch. That's for her chainsaw and her weed eater." I glanced back at him again as I said, "You never answered my question, though. Who do you think killed Bones?"

"I can't say for sure, but if I had to put money on it, I'd have to say that Marty did it."

His declaration startled me. "Is there any reason you feel that way?"

"He's the only one of us who could do it and not show any outward sign of regret afterward," Henry said. "If Gretchen or Peggy had done it, they'd be exhibiting at least some kind of remorse by now."

"Because they're women?"

"No, because they're human," Henry said.

"And Marty's not?"

"I don't know that I'd say that, but there's something cold about him that I can't put my finger on. I don't know, maybe I'm just jumping at shadows. All I know for sure is that I didn't do it."

We were back with the others now, and as we put the wood down near the fire, I looked at it and said, "One more load ought to do it. Marty, you're up."

"Whatever," Marty said, and we headed back to the woodpile for more firewood.

Once we were out of earshot of the others, I asked him, "Do you have any idea who might have killed Bones?"

"Henry," he said flatly.

"Really? Why?"

Marty studied me for a moment before speaking. "He probably just told you that I did it, didn't he?"

"I'm not comfortable commenting on that one way or the other," I said.

"You don't have to. I know the way his mind works, Pat. It would be the easiest thing in the world for him to blame me for it. If I were in his shoes, I'd probably say the same thing."

"You are in your own shoes, and you blamed him. I'd love to know why."

"Bones was hitting on Peggy, and it was obvious that he was taking a pretty hard run at her. Henry might seem like a nice, levelheaded guy, but I've seen him get jealous before. And then there's the treasure itself. If Bones found something and Henry knew about it, Bones wouldn't be safe."

"Are we talking about the same guy?" I asked. His portrayal of Henry was at odds with what I'd seen myself so far.

"I know, he seems like a really nice guy on the surface, but underneath that, there's a shark there, hiding from most of the world."

"How is it that you can see that side of him when other people can't?" I asked him.

"Maybe I've got a touch of the shark in me as well," Marty said with a chilling smile.

"Let's take greed out of the picture for a moment. Do you see either of the women killing Bones?"

"Of course I can. It's not that hard to swing a pickaxe."

"Maybe not," I countered, "but it has to be tough to plunge one into a person's back, especially more than once."

"I don't know what your experience in the world has been, but from what I've seen, women tend to be a lot more violent than men. They just don't show it as overtly."

"So, you can see Gretchen or Peggy killing Bones, is that right?"

"If he tried to force himself on one of them, you bet I could. I'm just surprised they didn't stab him more times than they did."

"Do you ever have any trouble sleeping at night, always expecting the worst from the people around you?" I asked him.

"Me? I sleep like a baby. That's what a clear conscience will do for you." It was one of those rare moments that Marty actually smiled and meant it.

We got another batch of firewood and headed back. "You know, just because we knew Bones, that doesn't mean that it was one of us that killed him," Marty said. "Money will make folks do things they'd never consider doing otherwise, and I'm sure there's no shortage of potential killers in your safe little town, no matter what you think, given the right motivation."

"We're considering that," I said, not realizing that I was giving too much away.

Marty grinned. "I'm minoring in psych. So, you and your twin sister are trying to solve Bones's murder, aren't you?"

"I don't suppose there's any use asking you to keep that to yourself," I said.

"Sure. Why not? It should be fun to watch you two at work tonight."

If I hadn't been certain before, I knew now that I wouldn't be sleeping for quite some time. This man was as unpredictable and potentially deadly as anyone I'd ever met.

We were nearly back to the fire pit when my cellphone rang. I put my wood down on the ground and saw that it was Darrel. Had he heard from Carter Hayes after all? "Sorry, but I've got to take this. Do you mind going back alone?"

"Got it," Marty said. "Thanks for the chat."

"You're welcome," I said. "Hey, Darrel, what's up?"

"Carter's here, but you can't tell anyone," he said softly.

"Does he know you're calling me?"

"No, of course not. If he did, he'd just run again. He's been ranting and raving about someone trying to kill him, and he asked me for a loan on top of what I just paid him, too."

"Why does he need so much money?" I asked him. "You made it sound as though he had a fair amount of cash."

"He does, but he still doesn't think it's going to be enough. I think he knows something, but he's too scared to tell me about it. Pat, he didn't kill that college student. I'd bet my life on it."

"In a way, you are. If Carter is a murderer, you could be putting yourself in danger right now."

"That should tell you just how sure I am," Darrel said. "He kept saying that there was no amount of money in the world worth the trouble he was in. He saw that young man get murdered from the trees, and when he ran away, he was pretty sure that the killer saw him, too."

"Did he say who did it?" I asked, trying my best not to glance over at the group, each member of which was currently closely watching me.

"No, he said that he couldn't make out the face," Darrel said.

"Was it a man or a woman at least?"

"I'm pretty sure that he knows, but he won't tell me," Darrel said. "All I could get out of him was that it was one of those four students. I'll keep working on him, but I wanted you to at least know that he was here."

"Thanks. Call me back, any time day or night, if you get anything else out of him."

"Will do," he said. "Pat, you and Annie need to watch your backs."

"We are," I said, and then I hung up.

"Who was that?" Annie asked me after I picked up the firewood and returned to the group.

"It was Jenna. She's going to be out of town a little longer," I lied.

"Who's Jenna?" Henry asked.

"She's my girlfriend," I said.

"I wish they'd come up with a better name than girlfriend when you've reached a certain age," Gretchen said. "It all sounds like grade school."

"They have other terms for adults," Peggy said.

"I know, but I don't like any of them, either."

"Maybe you should come up with something yourself," Marty suggested.

"How about paramour?" she asked. "I always thought that had a nice ring to it."

"Too French," Marty said. "Lover?"

"No. Just no," Peggy said.

"SO?" Gretchen asked.

"So what?" Marty asked.

"No. Significant Other. SO."

"It's too confusing," Henry said. "It will never catch on."

How had we gotten so far off topic? I interrupted by saying, "I'm just happy to have someone in my life I care about. The term 'girlfriend' is just fine with me."

Annie breathed in deeply, and then she said, "I think dinner's ready. Who's hungry?"

Everyone admitted that they were starving, so she lifted the lid of her Dutch oven and stuck a temperature probe into one of the chunks of beef. "It's perfect," Annie said as she grabbed a heavy fireproof glove and dumped the coals off the top of the pot before replacing it. Picking the pot up by its wire handle, she moved it to the picnic table and placed it in the center. "Let's eat."

CHAPTER 23: ANNIE

"That stew was delicious," Gretchen said as she finished eating. "How do you make it all taste so good?"

"I like to think that the outdoors makes it special," I said.

"Don't kid yourself. It's a lot harder than she makes it look. It's one thing to set the temperature on an oven but quite another to manage coals for so long to get the perfect outcome," Pat said.

"Thanks for the compliment," I said.

"Any chance for seconds?" Marty asked as he offered his cleaned plate.

"Absolutely," I answered, pleased that they all enjoyed my cooking. I knew in my heart that one of them was a killer, but that didn't stop me from taking everyone's compliments at face value. If that made me shallow, then so be it.

Henry and Gretchen each had a little more, while Peggy passed. I didn't hold it against her, though. After all, she hadn't been out of the hospital that long.

"Do you need any help cleaning up, Annie?" Pat asked me after we'd all had our fill of stew.

"Thanks, but I just need to save what's left, and then I'll clean up my Dutch oven. The rest can wait until later."

"I can at least help carry in the dirty dishes," Henry offered.

"We'll help, too," Gretchen volunteered.

"Why not? Everybody who wants to help should grab something, and we'll all head off to the cabin kitchen."

I grabbed the lid and pot, while Henry, Gretchen, and Peggy

gathered up everything else. Henry got to the door first, but he had a difficult time with it. "It's locked."

"Try pulling it instead of pushing," I said.

"The door opens outward? Why?"

"I know it's pretty unconventional, but it saves on floor space inside, something I have a definite lack of."

Henry pulled the door open, and the rest of us went inside.

The sink was loaded with the dirty dishes after I cleaned out the pot. Grabbing the olive oil and a few paper towels, I took the oven back outside, and soon enough, I had it dried and seasoned and ready to be put away until the next time I needed it.

Now it was time for the fun part.

"That's a really nice fire," I said as I took a seat.

"I thought it might be nice to have a little bonfire after that meal," Pat replied. "Is that okay with you?"

"I think it's a spectacular idea," I said.

Once we were all seated, I decided it was time to stir things up a little. "So you're all going back to school tomorrow. It's going to be hard, isn't it?"

"What do you mean?" Gretchen asked me.

"Well, chances are good that one of you killed Bones," I said as lightly as I could manage. "Once you're all away from here, I'm guessing that someone is going to get away with murder."

"What a terrible thing to say," Peggy said.

"It's true, though, isn't it?" Pat asked. "How are you going to deal with always being a suspect in Bones's murder for the rest of your life? That's a cloud that you'll never escape."

"No one thinks I did it!" Gretchen snapped.

"Come on, Gretchen," Peggy said. "You were furious when Bones made a pass at you, and you know it."

"He made a pass at you?" Marty asked her.

"Of course he did, and don't pretend that you didn't know it," Henry said.

"I didn't!"

"So you say," Henry added.

"He made a pass at you, too, Peggy," Gretchen said. "Don't bother denying it."

Peggy glanced at Henry, who was shaking his head. She couldn't just let it go, though. "I didn't kill him for doing it, though."

"You keep claiming that you found Bones dead in the pit. How can we be sure that you didn't kill him and then just claim to find the body to divert suspicion from yourself?" Gretchen asked, an ugly side coming to light in the campfire flames.

"If I killed him, then why would I tell anybody about it, let alone move the body to make myself look like a liar when I brought everyone out to see?"

"It's simple, and a little more clever than I ever gave you credit for. You wanted to muddy the waters and confuse things," Gretchen said.

"You mean like you're doing right now?" Henry asked her softly.

"What do you mean by that?"

"It just seems to me as though you're protesting an awful lot," he said.

"Henry, you had a reason to kill him yourself, so don't go getting all high and mighty on the rest of us. I heard that you were in more debt that anyone else and that you might have to drop out of school, so if Bones did find some of that money, you might have killed him for it yourself."

"I don't know where you're getting your information, but it's wrong nonetheless," Henry said.

"Even if Bones didn't find a dime, you still might kill him in anger for making a pass at Peggy. Everyone knows you've got a massive crush on her," Marty snapped.

"Whether he does or not, that doesn't make him a killer," Peggy said as she looked sympathetically at Henry, "any more than the fact that you've got a crush on Gretchen, which could have easily given you a motive for murder yourself."

"It's just a passing infatuation," Gretchen said, doing her best to discount his feelings for her.

"Actually, I'm pretty sure that it's the real deal," Marty admitted softly.

"You just think that you're feeling something for me," Gretchen said equally softly. "But you never pursued it. If you truly fancied me, you would have done something about it. So why didn't you?"

"Because I've seen the way you've been looking at Henry since we got here. There was no way I was going to put myself out there like that."

"That's not true!" she said.

"Come on. It's a fact, and you know it," Marty said as he looked at Peggy and then at Henry. "You guys have seen it, too, haven't you?"

At the exact time that Henry said no, Peggy answered yes.

"You knew?" he asked Peggy.

"You didn't?" Peggy asked Henry.

We were getting a little sidetracked, and I was about to rein us all back in when I heard the distinct sound of a branch cracking just outside the light of our fire.

"What was that?" I asked Pat.

"I don't know," he said as he stood, "but I'm going to find out."

As he started in the direction where the noise had come from, everyone else jumped up, too. Whoever had been spying on us understood that they'd lost the element of surprise. As they ran away from us into the woods, we could hear branches and twigs snapping furiously.

In the darkness, we lost whoever it was, and by the time we all made it back to the campfire, it was ebbing to mostly just embers.

"We're all here, so who could that have been out there spying on us, and more importantly, why?" Henry asked me.

"I don't have a clue," I admitted.

"It was your sister, wasn't it?" he asked again.

"If Kathleen was there, it's a surprise to us both," Pat replied.

Henry didn't look as though he believed it, and I couldn't say that I blamed him. He might even have been right. Had our big sister been spying on us? If she had been, I hoped that she didn't come back. Everyone was on edge now, and I had a feeling that the session of campfire confessions was over.

Peggy confirmed it by yawning as she stretched. "I'm beat. Is there any chance I can go ahead and hit the hay?"

"We'll all go in," Henry said. "It's getting late, and we have to get an early start tomorrow morning."

"I've got marshmallows, if anyone would like s'mores," I offered lamely.

"Thanks, but I couldn't eat another bite," Marty said as he slapped his stomach.

"I'm tired, too," Gretchen added.

"Okay. Pat, would you take care of putting out the fire? I'll take everyone else and get started inside."

"I'll lend him a hand," Henry volunteered.

"Thanks, but I can handle it myself," Pat offered.

"No offense, but what if whoever was out there decides to come back? I don't think any of us should be alone right now."

"That's a good point. Okay. Sure. You can help," Pat said.

I led the others inside the cabin as Pat and Henry worked at making sure the fire was completely extinguished, and I'd just gotten them all set up when I heard something loud bang against the outside door.

Someone had taken a chair and had wedged it against the door handle. No matter how hard I pushed, it wouldn't budge.

Had that same someone already done something to Pat and Henry?

And were they about to come after the rest of us now?

I was about to bolt out the back way when I saw a face looming in the window, wearing an expression that sent terror shooting through me.

We were in trouble, and lots of it.

"Henry, what's going on?" I asked the historian.

"Do you mean to tell me that you haven't figured it out by now?" he asked me with a wicked grin.

"Where's Pat?" I asked, doing my best to keep the terror out of my voice.

"No worries. He's close by," Henry said, "and before any of you get the smart idea of sneaking out the back door, I took care of that earlier. There's no way out."

"Or in, either," I said. "Pat? Pat!"

There was no answer.

"What did you do to my brother?" I was in full panic mode now, and I didn't care who knew it.

"He's taking a little nap, unless I hit him too hard with that piece of firewood and it's a little more permanent," Henry said casually. "I was going to take one of the coins I got off Bones's body and use it to frame one of the others, but I couldn't pass up the perfect opportunity to get rid of you all at once."

"Why would you want to hurt us?" Peggy asked, crying as she spoke. "You like me."

"Sure I do, but with what Bones found, I don't need you anymore. I have a feeling that I won't have any shortage of girlfriends once I cash the treasure in."

"Is that why you killed him?" I asked, hoping to stall long enough for either Pat to wake up or Kathleen to come check on us. It wasn't much, but it was the best I could do.

"If he'd just handed the coins over to me, I wouldn't have had to do *anything* to him," Henry said. "If you look at it one way, it was his fault, not mine."

This kid had clearly gone around the bend. "But why do anything now? We didn't know you killed Bones. You could have just walked out of here tomorrow and gotten away with it."

"And have that cloud of guilt hanging over me for the rest of my life? No thank you. This way is better. By the time I'm finished telling my story, I'm going to be the hero who tried to save you all. It's going to be perfect."

"Not for us, you jerk," Marty snapped.

"Careful there, Marty," Henry said. "You don't want to make me angry."

"Why not? You're out there, and we're in here." He grabbed a lamp and gestured menacingly with it. "Come on in and find out what we'll do to you if you try anything."

"That's the beauty of it. I don't have to," Henry said, and then he showed us something that terrified me yet again.

It was my gasoline can, and I knew for a fact that it was nearly full.

"Open the window and throw your phones out."

"No way," Marty said. "I'm calling the cops."

"That's fine, but ask yourself a question first. Do you want to die fast or slow?" Henry asked. There was no doubt in my mind that he was capable of killing us all.

"Do as he says," I said, dialing Kathleen's number as I opened the window and threw my phone out, hoping that she'd pick up and hear what was going on.

The others grumbled, but they followed suit. Kathleen was close by. At least she had been before we'd caught her spying on us.

I just hoped she'd get to us in time.

"Don't do it, Henry," I begged. I had no desire to burn to death.

"It's for the best," he said as he motioned for me to close the window I'd just opened. "And don't try to break a window and get out. I've got a gun, so you're not going to make it out alive either way. Trust me, you don't want to die by gunshot."

"Do you think burning alive is any better?" Gretchen asked defiantly.

"I don't know. I'll ask you in a few minutes," he said as he started to slosh gasoline around on the porch.

"Why move the body?" I asked him loudly, trying to get him to stop what he was doing.

"Like I said before, it was to muddy the waters," he replied, still sloshing gasoline everywhere. "It worked, too. I'm not going to stand here chatting with you while you wait for someone to come to your rescue. It's time to die."

It appeared that we had run out of time.

I only hoped our demise was as painless as Pat's had been, if he was indeed dead.

But I doubted it.

He most likely hadn't known what hit him, but I had a feeling that we'd feel every second of it ourselves.

CHAPTER 24: PAT

WHEN I CAME TO, I heard voices, and for a second, I thought it was all in my mind.

Then I looked around and saw Henry spreading gasoline on my sister's front porch. As I tried to stand, I stumbled backward. My head was screaming with pain, and blood had dripped into my eyes while I'd been unconscious. Steadying myself, I picked up the piece of firewood I assumed Henry had clubbed me in the face with and started toward the porch, dying a little with each step. I felt as though I was about to throw up, but I fought the feeling. After this was over, if any of us lived through it, I'd have plenty of time to be sick. Right now, my twin needed me, and I was going to save her, even if I died in the process.

I was within six feet of him when I stepped on a twig I hadn't seen before.

Henry whirled around, and I launched the log in my hand at his head.

Unfortunately, I missed.

Henry dropped the gasoline can, and I could smell it in the air as it spilled out onto the ground.

"I thought I already took care of you once," Henry said with obvious distaste.

"No such luck," I said as I looked around for something else to throw at him.

Annie screamed from inside, "Look out, Pat! He's got a gun!"

At that point, it really didn't matter. The only way I might get away from him was to run into the shadows of the woods around Annie's place, but if I did that, I'd be sealing four death warrants, so even if I survived, I knew that I wouldn't feel much like living any more.

Trying my best to ignore the pain and my difficulty in staying upright, I ran straight at Henry, bracing myself for the impact of the first bullet.

As I threw myself at him, I heard the window shatter, but by then, it was probably going to be too late.

At least someone else might be able to grab the gun after he killed me.

It would be something, anyway.

To my surprise, I didn't feel any slugs ripping into my body. My hands wrapped around Henry's neck, and I found myself on top of him, squeezing as hard as I could.

Someone pulled me off, but I couldn't say who had done it.

I had been in some kind of altered state, and only Henry's life would have appeased my lust for his death. I quickly came back to reality as Annie leaned over me and hugged me. "You saved us."

"Did you get his gun?" I asked, barely able to breathe now for some reason.

"He didn't have one. He was bluffing," Marty said.

"Did I...did I kill him?" I asked hoarsely.

"No, but he's unconscious," Gretchen said. "His pulse is strong though, and he's breathing just fine. He might have a little laryngitis after this, but that should be about it."

"Good. That's good," I said as I heard a siren heading up Annie's road, and that was the last thing I remembered as I felt myself sinking into a dark abyss.

"Where am I?" I asked as I opened my eyes. "Hospital," I said, answering my own question as I felt my head wound. It had been cleaned up and bandaged, and the pain had eased quite a bit. "I feel better."

"With what they've got you on, you shouldn't be feeling anything at all," Annie said from my bedside.

"How's Henry? Is he awake?"

"Short of a raspy voice, he's going to be fine. He's suing you for assault, by the way," Annie said with a grin.

"Of course he is. Did he have the treasure on him?"

"Some of it. The kids don't think it was anywhere near what Blankenship's journal promised, but Kathleen's satisfied that the rest of it was uncovered long ago. All in all, Peggy estimated it to be worth around ten thousand dollars in gold and silver."

"Bones died for that little?" I asked.

"A great deal of men and women have died for far less," she said. "I called Jenna. She'll be here in a few hours."

"I didn't mean for her to cut her trip short," I said.

"I tried to tell her that you wouldn't want her to do that, but she refused to listen to me."

"Good girl," I said, getting a little groggy from the medication, no doubt.

"Which one of us?" Annie asked me as I started to slip away again.

"Both," I mumbled, and then I was gone again.

CHAPTER 25: ANNIE

"**H**ow is he?" Timothy asked me breathlessly as he rushed up to me outside my brother's hospital room. They'd decided that Pat needed his rest, but that was as far as they'd been able to get me to move, and I wasn't about to cede another inch.

"He's going to be fine," I said. "Thank goodness for that thick skull of his."

"I always thought that was one of his finest qualities," Timothy answered. "I'm so sorry, Annie."

"About what?" I asked him, afraid to show any emotion for fear of breaking down completely.

"How about a blanket apology that covers everything since those kids started digging up my land?" he asked me.

"I can do that," I said, feeling a smile blossom on my lips.

"Is it really going to be that easy?" he asked.

"What do you think?" I asked him with a grin.

"I believe that this is the first of many apologies I'll be making in the near future," he said as he leaned over and kissed me.

It was the best way I knew for him to guarantee my forgiveness, not that I wasn't still planning on making him squirm a little before I let him off the hook entirely.

"I'm sorry that I wasn't there for you," Timothy said as he pulled another chair over beside mine. "To think that something almost happened to you while I was off pouting is just about more than I can take."

"It didn't, though," I said. "I'm fine."

"Thanks to Pat."

"Hey, I didn't just stand there waiting to be rescued," I said.

"I know."

"Do you want to know the truth? It was all my brother, every last bit of it. Even though he thought Henry had a gun, he still threw himself at the man like a lunatic. It was kind of heroic to watch, to be honest with you."

"I'm not surprised."

"Really? Because it shocked the daylights out of me," I answered with a grin.

"You would have done the same thing for him, and you know it," Timothy said.

"I hope so, but then again, I'd just as soon not get the chance." Something had been nagging me for a while, but I'd never had a chance to mention it to Timothy. "By the way, I agree with the kids."

"About what?"

"There's a great deal more money to be found on your land if we just know where to look," I said.

"How do you figure that?"

"Pat showed me a few pictures he took earlier at the old homestead, and I think I figured out where Jonas hid the bulk of his money."

Timothy looked askance at me. "Annie, we don't need to talk about this right now."

"Why not? It's going to be hours before Pat wakes up again." I grabbed my brother's phone, something I'd taken when he'd first been brought in, and I opened up the photos he'd taken. It took me a minute to get to the right one, and then I showed it to Timothy. "You should look for the real money there."

"No way. You've got to be kidding."

"Apparently old Jonas had a sense of humor, at least according to the kids," I said with a smile. "If you take a few flashlights with you, you should be able to find out tonight."

"I'm not going anywhere," he said as he reached out and took my hand.

"I suppose it's waited this long, so it can at least wait until morning."

"It's going to have to wait longer than that," Timothy said. "When Pat gets discharged, the three of us will look together."

"What if someone else gets there first?" I asked him.

"I can live with that. What I can't live with is the thought that this stupid money almost came between us. If that's the cost of finding it, I'd just as soon leave it exactly where it is right now."

And then he kissed me again, and suddenly, I forgot all about the money.

CHAPTER 26: PAT

"I FEEL LIKE A GHOUL DOING this," I said four days later. I'd been discharged by then, and when Timothy and Annie had explained their plans to me, I'd pushed it back a few more days until I could at least help with the digging, too.

"If I'm right," Annie said, "we're not desecrating anything."

"But if you're wrong?" I asked as the shovel bit into the red clay again.

"Then it's going to be an unhappy surprise for the bones of Mr. Cash," she said.

"I still can't believe it was right under everyone's noses the entire time," I said as I lifted out another shovel full of dirt.

"Hey, it's my turn," Timothy said. "I want to dig some, too."

"One more load," I promised. "If Henry had gotten Jonas's sense of humor when he'd first read that journal, he'd have known right where to look."

"Let's just hope that we're right," Timothy said.

"Does the money mean that much to you?" Annie asked him.

"I won't turn it down if we find any, but the fact that we're all here doing it together is all that I need to make me smile."

I shoved the blade of the shovel a little deeper, and felt it contact something hard. "Guys, I might have something here."

I dug a little more carefully, and soon enough, I had unearthed a small, coffin-shaped metal box. "What happened? Did he bury his pet squirrel here?" Annie asked me.

I handed the box to Timothy. "If he did, you're about to get a big surprise."

Timothy took the box, and then he hesitated a moment before he opened it. "If there's anything in here, I want you two to have half of it."

"What are we going to do with half of a squirrel skeleton?" Annie asked him.

"I'm talking about money," Timothy said.

"Half is too much," I said. "Right, Annie?"

"Of course it is," she said. "How about ten percent?"

"Annie!"

"What? Don't we at least deserve a finder's fee, Pat?" she asked me.

"I don't know about that," I said.

"Let's open the box and see if there's anything even worth discussing first," she said.

"I can live with that," Timothy said. It took him a few moments, but he finally managed to pry off the lid.

There were several gold and silver coins inside, but most of it had once been paper money. Water had gotten into it over time, and it was all nearly rotted away.

"It's not exactly a fortune," I said.

"No, but it was cash indeed. Jonas didn't lie," Timothy said with a grin. "There's still some real value here."

"Enough to build that cabin you've been dreaming about, especially if you use all of it?" Annie asked him.

"What about your finder's fee?" he asked.

"I can live with my share going to a good cause; what about you, Pat?"

"I think it's a splendid idea," I said.

"Then that's what I'll do," Timothy said. "Thank you both."

"It is our pleasure," I said as I offered him my hand.

"Forget about a handshake," Annie said. "I want a kiss."

"You can have mine, too," I said with a grin.

In the end, it had all worked out for the best.

At least for everyone except Bones and Henry.

Once again, greed had played a part in murder.

Annie and I didn't have much, at least not monetarily, but we had each other and other people who cared about us as well, including our big sister and our significant others.

To us, it was the richest that either one of us had ever hoped to be in all of our lives.

And that was more than enough.

RECIPES

Annie's Cast Iron Pork Roast

We discovered this meal when pork roast was on sale at our local grocery store. For half off the regular price, this frugal shopper wasn't about to pass up a deal like that! After returning home, I glanced through half a dozen recipes, but I wasn't satisfied with the standard rosemary and/or basil combos I found. I cooked my roast in my Dutch oven, even given that it was a very different cut of meat altogether, but I thought, why not? This recipe evolved from that first happy experiment, and I hope you like it. There are many variations to my basic recipe, so don't be afraid to use your imagination.

Ingredients

- 2 pounds boneless, center-cut pork roast
- 8–10 carrots, peeled and cut into chunks
- 1 large onion, cut radially to produce rings
- 6 red new potatoes or 1 large baking potato
- 1 bottle barbeque sauce (18 ounces), divided into quarters
- 1 can beef broth, 14.5 ounces (apple cider or wine can be substituted if you'd like, but I always use broth. I like the flavor and moisture beef broth gives, but I suppose you could use chicken or vegetable broth if you'd like.)

Directions

Four to twenty-four hours ahead of time, score the top of the pork roast (where the fat is located) diagonally, approximately two inches apart and two inches deep, intersecting the lines. Take half of the barbeque sauce (approximately nine ounces or two quarters) and rub it into the top, making sure to get sauce down into the scored openings. Seal the pork in a large gallon-sized baggie, or put it into a large mixing bowl, cover it with plastic wrap, and let it marinate at least four hours in the refrigerator.

Thirty to forty minutes before you're ready to put it in the oven, take it out of the refrigerator and let the roast warm up a bit before cooking.

Preheat your oven to 325 degrees F. While you're waiting for it to come to temperature, cut the vegetables as directed into large chunks and spread them out on the bottom of the Dutch oven. Add the broth now so you don't splash off any of the sauce still remaining from the marinade. The onions should be ringed (cut in full or partial rings), while the carrots and potato should be cut into 2 – or 3-inch chunks. Lay the pork roast over the vegetables and apply one quarter of the sauce over the top. As always, the purpose of the vegetables is twofold: to keep the meat from burning on the bottom and to add a delicious side to the meal.

Put the lid on the Dutch oven and cook for approximately two hours, or until a meat thermometer in the center of the meat reads 160 to 165 degrees F. While it's true that in many cases, 145 degrees F is now the approved minimum internal temperature for pork, I like mine without pink throughout.

Your results may vary, and the author wishes you the best, while taking no responsibility, implied or otherwise, for your health.

After two to two and a half hours, check the temperature and adjust your time accordingly. Once the roast is to your preferred level of doneness (see disclaimer above), pull everything out of the Dutch oven and place it on a serving plate, cover with foil, and let rest for fifteen to twenty minutes. Serve while hot, and enjoy.

Yields a meal for four people

Pat's Sausage Mash-Up

Yes, it's true. Pat can cook with cast iron, too! This is a favorite around my house and simple to make as well. You could use one cast iron skillet if you'd like, browning the meat first, setting it aside, and then sautéing the vegetables and mushrooms, but it's twice as fast if you use two skillets! This is a hearty meal and goes particularly well with artisan bread or as a stuffing for omelets.

Ingredients

- 1 pound ground pork farmhouse-style sausage (Italian can be substituted if preferred)
- 1 green bell pepper, chopped
- 1 medium onion, chopped (white, yellow, or Vidalia)
- 8 ounces baby Portobello mushrooms, sliced
- 1/4 stick butter, melted
- 1/4 cup olive oil
- 12 ounces Monterey jack/Colby cheese blend, shredded (feel free to substitute any cheese you prefer)

Directions

In one pan, brown the sausage, and in another, melt the butter and heat the oil together. This combination gives great flavor and a higher smoking point than butter alone. Add the diced onion and green pepper, as well as the sliced mushrooms. While the sausage is browning, sauté the vegetables and mushrooms until they are softened. Add the medley to the sausage and then top with cheese. Bake in a 400 degree F oven for 10 minutes.

Serve these while hot, and enjoy.

Yields a meal for three to four people

If you enjoy Jessica Beck Mysteries and you would like to be notified when the next book is being released, please send your email address to newreleases@jessicabeckmysteries.net. Your email address will not be shared, sold, bartered, traded, broadcast, or disclosed in any way. There will be no spam from us, just a friendly reminder when the latest book is being released.

Also, be sure to visit our website at jessicabeckmysteries.net for valuable information about Jessica's books.

OTHER BOOKS BY JESSICA BECK

The Donut Mysteries

Glazed Murder
Fatally Frosted
Sinister Sprinkles
Evil Éclairs
Tragic Toppings
Killer Crullers
Drop Dead Chocolate
Powdered Peril
Illegally Iced
Deadly Donuts
Assault and Batter
Sweet Suspects
Deep Fried Homicide
Custard Crime
Lemon Larceny
Bad Bites
Old Fashioned Crooks
Dangerous Dough
Troubled Treats
Sugar Coated Sins
Criminal Crumbs

The Classic Diner Mysteries

A Chili Death
A Deadly Beef
A Killer Cake
A Baked Ham
A Bad Egg
A Real Pickle
A Burned Biscuit

The Ghost Cat Cozy Mysteries
Ghost Cat: Midnight Paws
Ghost Cat 2: Bid for Midnight

The Cast Iron Cooking Mysteries
Cast Iron Will
Cast Iron Conviction
Cast Iron Cover-Up

Made in the USA
San Bernardino, CA
21 March 2016